THE TEXAS BROTHERHOOD

Home to Texas and straight to the altar!

A home. A family. A legacy of their own.

Mustang Valley has long been home to the brotherhood. United by blood, trust and loyalty, these men fight for what they believe—for family, for what's right and ultimately…for love.

Now there are newcomers in their midst. Two gorgeous new Randell brothers are back to reclaim their heritage, find their family and just maybe discover the women of their dreams….

**In January,
Luke Randell returned and claimed a wife in**
Luke: The Cowboy Heir

**Now his brother's back!
But is this rebel ready to wed?
Find out in**
Brady: The Rebel Rancher

Dear Reader,

I'm so pleased that I have the opportunity to return to Mustang Valley and revisit the Randell men from my TEXAS BROTHERHOOD series. You will want to find out what Jack Randell's boys Chance, Cade and Travis have been up to. Along with their half brothers Jared Trager and Wyatt and Dylan Gentry, they have all adjusted to the valley. I'm here to say that they're all doing well, including Hank Barrett, the adopted patriarch of the family.

My inspiration for this series and Hank's character was my dear friend Hence Barrow, a West Texas rancher. He's the one who taught this city girl all about ranching. I'm sorry to say Hence passed away in 2007, just a few months shy of his ninety-eighth birthday, but I'll never forget his stories and his love of the land. It was an honor and a privilege to know him, and to be called his friend. I'll miss you, Hence.

In this series I bring Jack's brother Sam Randell's sons, Luke and Brady, to the valley. In this story, F-16 pilot Captain Brady Randell is injured on a mission and comes home to the Rocking R Ranch. While recuperating he gets to know his half brother and the rest of the Randell cousins. He also tangles with an independent female veterinarian, Lindsey Stafford, who has secrets of her own. In the end they both want the same thing—to be a part of the Randell family.

There are many more surprises. I hope you enjoy it.

With regards,

Patricia Thayer

PATRICIA THAYER

Brady: The Rebel Rancher

THE
TEXAS
BROTHERHOOD

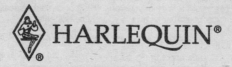

HARLEQUIN®

TORONTO • NEW YORK • LONDON
AMSTERDAM • PARIS • SYDNEY • HAMBURG
STOCKHOLM • ATHENS • TOKYO • MILAN • MADRID
PRAGUE • WARSAW • BUDAPEST • AUCKLAND

Recycling programs
for this product may
not exist in your area.

ISBN-13: 978-0-373-17571-0
ISBN-10:   0-373-17571-X

BRADY: THE REBEL RANCHER

Originally published in the U.K. in 2009 as
THE REBEL HEIR'S BRIDE.

First North American Publication 2009.

Copyright © 2009 by Patricia Wright.

Printed in U.S.A.

Patricia Thayer has been writing for more than twenty years, and has published thirty books with Harlequin®. Her books have been nominated for various awards in the U.S. including the National Readers' Choice Award, the Book Buyers' Best and a prestigious RITA® Award. In 1997, *Nothing Short of a Miracle* won the *Romantic Times BOOKreviews* Reviewers' Choice Award for Best Special Edition.

Thanks to the understanding men in her life— her husband of more than thirty-five years, Steve, and her three grown sons and three grandsons— Pat has been able to fulfill her dream of writing. Besides writing romance fiction, she loves to travel—especially in the West, where she researches her books firsthand. You might find her on a ranch in Texas or on a train to an old mining town in Colorado, and this year you'll find her on an adventure in Scotland. Just so long as she can share it all with her favorite hero, Steve. She loves to hear from readers. You can write to her at P.O. Box 6251, Anaheim, California 92816-0251, U.S.A., or check her Web site at www.patriciathayer.com for upcoming books.

**Don't miss Patricia Thayer's
next Harlequin Romance**
The Cowboy's Baby
July 2009

To the newest addition to the family,
Finley Steven. Hero material for sure. And to his
mother, Daralynn. You never stop amazing me.

Thank you for another fine grandson.

CHAPTER ONE

HE'D always been told he was too cocky for his own good.

On a sunny November morning, Brady Randell hobbled out to the porch with the aid of a crutch. His left leg was bandaged from his last surgery and covered in a removable cast strapped from his foot up over his knee to his thigh. It served to protect the damaged bone so it could heal properly. If it ever did. Three months since the accident, and he wasn't feeling so damn cocky anymore.

With a groan Brady dropped into the Adirondack chair. This was about as far as he traveled these days. He was tired of doing nothing but sleeping, eating and sitting around. Oh, yeah, he forgot about going to therapy twice a week. Or maybe he should call it torture.

After all his hard work, he hoped for a payoff, some good news when he saw the doctor next week. With a little luck he could get the cast off and finally be able to walk on his own again.

"Wouldn't that be a miracle," he murmured in frustration.

He sighed, recalling the vivid details of the accident that had caused him to drop right out of the sky. He'd barely had time to eject from the cockpit before the crash of his F-16.

Brady tensed. He could still feel the bone-bruising tremors; hear the death screams of the powerful aircraft disintegrating as it plowed into the desert floor. He'd gone over and over in his head what he could have done differently. What had gone so terribly wrong that day?

Was this possibly the end of Captain "Rebel" Randell's air force career?

Now instead of being in the cockpit of the Fighting Falcon, he was parked on a porch of the foreman's house outside San Angelo, Texas. His daddy's home, the Rocking R Ranch. After Sam Randell's death, it now belonged to him and his half brother, Luke, who, after thirty years, he'd finally met. Since the accident, Brady had needed a place to heal. He thought a remote, inherited ranch would be perfect for a loner like him.

Brady stared out toward the barn and corral area where his new sister-in-law, Tess Randell, was working one of her horses in the large arena. She rode like nobody's business. Watching her skill and grace was the treat of his day. That and being left alone.

Brady closed his eyes and leaned back. Not that he was going to get any peace and quiet staying here. He had family coming out of the woodwork. Up at the main ranch house Luke lived with his bride and ready-made family—a young daughter, Livy, Tess's father, Ray, who had Alzheimer's and kept referring to Brady as Sam's boy. And Aunt Bernice, who spoke her mind and could cook up a storm.

They weren't so bad, but the six Randell cousins

who lived in the neighboring ranches with all their wives and kids were a bit much. And there were lots of kids. Evidently, there wasn't much else to do on the ranch during those long nights.

With a groan he shifted in his chair, recalling the last time he'd spent the night with a willing woman. It had been too long.

"Excuse me, are you all right?"

At the sound of a female voice, Brady's eyes shot open. He blinked and focused on a pair of big, emerald-green eyes staring back at him from the edge of the porch. They belonged to a ·petite woman dressed in snug jeans, a white blouse and a denim jacket. Her hair was the rich color of cinnamon, cut just at her jawline, and wayward strands brushed against her full lips. A black cowboy hat sat firmly on her head.

He swallowed the sudden dryness in his throat. "I'm fine," he told her.

"I heard you groan and—" she glanced down at his injured leg "—wondered if you were in pain."

Damn right he was. "I'm fine," he repeated.

She gave him a half smile and his heart began to race. "Then I apologize for disturbing you."

This woman could disturb a man in a coma. She looked like every man's dream. That was if you were into fiery redheads. Oh, yeah. He sat up straighter. "Are you lost or something?"

She looked around. "I'm here to see Tess Randell."

Brady glanced at the oversize case she was toting. Great, a solicitor out in the middle of nowhere. "If you're here to sell her something, she's busy."

The woman shook her head and raised an eyebrow. "Actually, I was invited. She called me."

"Right."

Her shoulders tensed. "If you'll just direct me to Tess Randell, I won't bother you any longer."

From the corner of his eye, Brady saw his sister-in-law hurrying toward them. "Looks like we'll both get our wish," he told the pretty intruder.

Tess rushed toward them. "Good, you found us," she said a little breathless. The statuesque blonde wore her long hair tired back in a ponytail. "Did you have much trouble with my directions?"

The redhead glanced at Brady. "Nothing I couldn't handle."

Smiling, Tess's gaze shifted to him. "Have you two met?"

Before Brady could speak, the woman said, "We haven't had a chance."

"Brady, this is Dr. Lindsey Stafford. She's the new veterinarian taking over Dr. Hillman's practice while he's recovering from his hip surgery. Be nice, or you'll have to answer to the Randell cousins, especially Travis. He went all the way to Dallas to find her." Tess turned to the redhead. "Lindsey, this is my brother-in-law, Brady Randell. He's a captain in the air force."

Lindsey fought her nervousness. Not because the man was drop-dead gorgeous, but every time she met another Randell she was afraid someone would figure out who she was.

"It was nice to meet you, Brady." She held out her hand.

He shook it. "Same here, Doc. You'll excuse me if I don't get up."

She nodded, not missing the sarcasm in his voice. "Hope you have a speedy recovery."

Those midnight eyes locked with hers. "Not nearly as much as I do."

"Well," Tess began, "I better take you down to the barn." She turned to Brady. "You need anything?"

"No, I can manage."

Tess nodded. "If you see Luke, tell him where I went. Come with me, Lindsey."

Lindsey quickly followed Tess along the path. She didn't want to have any more conversation with the man.

"Sorry about my brother-in-law," Tess began. "He's recovering from an accident and is a little antsy with his confinement. Of course, that doesn't excuse his rude behavior."

"You don't have to apologize for him. I'll just keep my distance next visit."

Tess Randell was beautiful to begin with, but when she smiled she was gorgeous. Tall, with long legs, her every movement was graceful. Everything Lindsey always wanted to be. But at twenty-nine she was resigned to the fact she'd stopped growing at five-foot-three, and her freckles across her nose would not suddenly vanish.

They arrived at the pristine white barn and walked inside. Lindsey looked around the well-kept area where new-looking stalls lined both walls. She followed Tess down the center aisle to a section that was designated as the grooming area. A stable boy was washing one of the horses.

They continued past three beautiful quarter horses that peered over their gates to see the visitors. "These are horses I board and train, and their owner has given me permission to call you if I feel the need."

"Good." Lindsey stopped to pet one of the equines. "I'd hate to think about something happening to one of these beautiful animals."

"That's the reason I'm so happy you came here to practice."

"I was lucky to get the chance." She walked alongside of Tess. "I don't have much experience yet, and this will definitely help build my résumé." And she never dreamed she would get the opportunity to meet the Randells. It was a chance she couldn't pass up.

"The vet you interned for in Ft. Worth gave you a glowing recommendation. That's good enough for us." They stopped at the stall of a young bay stallion. "This here is Smooth Whiskey Doc. He's my number-one concern. I hope to have him compete in the NCHA Futurity."

Lindsey was mesmerized by the beautiful golden bay horse. When she went to him, he showed no shyness and came to the gate to greet her. She set her case down and he immediately nudged her hand. When she rubbed his muzzle, he blew out a breath.

"I think I'm in love," Lindsey said with a big grin. But her thoughts suddenly turned to the brooding Brady Randell.

"Be careful," Tess warned. "He's fickle."

"I don't doubt that for a second," she said, remarking about both stallions.

Whiskey bobbed his head as if to agree and they

both laughed. All the time, Lindsey was looking the animal over. He was about sixteen hands high, his eyes were clear, and his coat shiny. Well cared for.

"What seems to be your problem, big boy?"

Tess swung open the gate and walked in beside the horse. Her hand smoothed over his withers across his back and down his rump. "It's probably minor, but I didn't want to take a chance with this guy." She talked soothingly as she leaned down to reveal the gash just below the hock on his hind leg.

"I was working him in a cutting exercise and he got clipped by a steer."

Lindsey ran her hand along the horse's rump as she crooned to him. She didn't want to get kicked because the animal was nervous. Tess did her part, too, to keep Whiskey still.

Lindsey examined the open wound closely, then asked, "When did it happen?"

"About a week ago. I've been treating it with the normal antiseptic cream and clean bandages."

"You were right to call me. In a few more days, this could have really gotten infected. I believe a strong dose of antibiotics will clear it up, but I want you to stop training for a few days."

Lindsey went to her bag. "I've looked over Dr. Hillman's file on Whiskey. He was examined just a month ago, but I'll give him a quick check just so I can get familiar with him."

Tess looked relieved. "That's fine with me."

After the exam, Lindsey gave Whiskey a glowing report. They came out of the stall in time to see a man walking down the aisle. He was tall with a muscular build, coal-black hair and a cleft chin. Obviously another Randell.

"Luke," Tess called, love shining in her eyes. "You're finished with the meeting already."

"Not exactly." He leaned down and kissed his wife, then looked at Lindsey. "Hello, you must be Dr. Stafford. I'm Luke Randell."

She nodded. So, another cousin to Jack's boys. "Lindsey, please. Nice to meet you." Oh, my, another charming Randell man. Suddenly Captain Brady Randell came into her head. Correction. Not all were charming. Some were just too damn good-looking.

Brady stood leaning against the porch post as he watched for the redheaded vet to come out of the barn. Hell, why not? How often did a pretty woman—who wasn't a Randell—come around? It was the most excitement he'd had in days. Besides, he had nothing better to do.

That wasn't exactly true.

He glanced toward the large house on the hill. There were several cars parked in the driveway, probably for another business meeting with Randell Corp. He'd been invited to attend, but he'd declined. He wasn't into numbers and budgets. That was his brother's show.

All Brady had to do was sit back and let everyone else handle things. Hadn't that been what he'd done since he arrived here? Just sit around and heal. Isn't that what he wanted? Silence and solitude so he could think?

He raked his fingers through his grown-out regulation military cut, then across the two-day beard along his jaw. He'd let himself go to hell. Suddenly he cared, because a woman showed up here.

The sound of laughter brought him back to reality. He looked toward the barn to see Luke and Tess, escorting the pretty vet down the path toward the house.

Great. Why hadn't he gone inside sooner. The last thing he wanted was for them to find him here. But before he could make his escape, his brother spotted him.

"Hey, Brady." He waved and they started to the porch.

He froze. "Hey, Luke."

They arrived all smiles and Brady suddenly felt left out. "Have you met Lindsey Stafford?"

He nodded, trying to balance his weight using the post. "We've met already."

The redhead looked up at Luke and smiled. "Brady mistook me for a salesperson."

"Really." Luke stood there looking smug.

Brady refused to let his brother outmaneuver him. He could sweet-talk as well as the next guy. "Well, Doc, no one said our new vet would look like you. I guess you could say I was blindsided."

Lindsey could see through Brady's sudden charming attitude. Well, she wasn't going to let him have the upper hand. "Believe me, it won't happen again," she told him, unable to understand why he seemed to dislike her so. "I should get back, Mr. Randell," she said, then turned away to go with Tess and Luke.

Before she could make her departure, she heard a curse and a thud. She swung around to find Brady Randell lying on the porch floor.

"Brady!" Luke called. He was the first to reach him. Lindsey followed behind him.

She knelt down beside Brady, who was lying flat on his back. He tried to raise his head, his face strained in pain. "No, stay where you are," she ordered.

He grimaced again. "Who made you the boss?"

"Are you going to fight me for the title?" She was eyeing the leg in a cast. "Did you twist your leg?"

"No, I fell on my arm, trying to catch myself," he said, still fighting her to sit up.

Once again, she pushed him back down. "Lie still," she ordered, then reached for his arm.

"What the hell are you doing?" He tried to pull away.

"I just can't resist you, Mr. Randell. So lie there and enjoy the attention."

Brady's angry gaze went to his brother, but Luke just held up his hand in surrender. "I suggest you listen to her."

"Then make it quick. And if you're going to get familiar, you can drop the mister." With a groan, he did as he was told.

Lindsey checked his arms and good leg, happy to find nothing broken. But she soon discovered a lump on the back of his head. She had him open those piercing brown eyes. Although they weren't dilated, he could still have a concussion.

She turned to Luke. "Seems nothing is broken. Could you help me get him on his feet and inside?"

"I don't need help, Doc," Brady continued to argue.

"Come on, Brady," his brother urged. "You need to listen, or I'm going to take you to the emergency room."

Brady grumbled and finally sat up. Lindsey couldn't help but notice his hard, flat stomach that his dark T-shirt didn't hide when his bomber jacket fell open. His chest and arms weren't bad, either. With Luke and

Lindsey gripping his arms, they managed to get him to his feet.

Lindsey immediately felt his strength, his power and his masculinity, too. The sudden feelings he evoked surprised her. He was definitely not her type of man. Too dangerous.

Tess handed Brady his crutch, and Luke helped his brother inside the cottage. Tess and Lindsey followed behind them and into a small living room that was cluttered with newspapers and magazines but clean otherwise.

"You want to go to your room or stay out here?" Luke asked.

Brady pulled away from his brother, made his way to the sofa and sat down. "I'm fine right here. So you all can leave."

Tess and Luke looked at Lindsey for confirmation.

"He's got a small lump on his head," she told them. "But his pupils aren't dilated."

"No concussion," Brady said. "So go."

Luke looked at his wife. "If you stay for thirty minutes, I can finish up the meeting and be back here."

"But Livy's bus is due," she said, and glanced at her watch.

"All of you go," Brady demanded. "I'll be fine alone."

"I can stay until you get back," Lindsey offered.

"Oh, thank you, Lindsey," Tess said. "I promise I'll be back soon as I pick up Livy."

"I'll get back as soon as the meeting is over. And I'm still thinking you should get checked out," Luke said, then followed his wife out the door.

Suddenly Lindsey was alone with this overbearing man.

"Well, now you're stuck," Brady said as he lifted his cast-covered leg onto the coffee table.

"I'm not stuck," she denied. "But it would be nice if you tried to be civil."

"Why should I? I just want to be left alone."

"And I'm sure you will be when your family learns you're okay. When do you see your doctor again?"

Brady started to say it was none of her business, but found he liked her being here, though not exactly under these circumstances. "In a few days."

"Let him know what happened today. In fact you should call him and tell him."

"Lady, that's not going to happen."

She gave him a stubborn look. "I'm not the enemy here, Brady. So you aren't going to run me off. Not until I want to leave. That will be when Tess comes back."

Brady studied her for a few minutes. Lindsey Stafford was different than most women who hung around the base. Those females were overeager to please the hot-shot pilots. This woman had a take-me-as-I-am-or-not-at-all attitude.

"Maybe I've been a little hard on you."

Those big eyes widened in surprise. "You think?"

"Okay, I plead guilty. Now please sit down. You're giving me neck strain from looking up at you."

She sank down in an overstuffed chair across from him. "That's a switch."

Brady felt his mouth twitch. "Get picked on for your size, huh?"

She glared. "Not since seventh grade."

"That's a lie," he said as his gaze combed over her petite body. "What do you weigh? A hundred pounds?"

"One hundred and ten. I work out to build muscle. The added strength helps in my profession."

He'd like to see those muscles. Dear Lord, he was pathetic. "Why aren't you working with dogs and cats? It would seem easier."

She shook her head. "I love horses. My mother and stepfather are horse breeders. I grew up around them."

"Where are you from?"

She hesitated for a second. "North of Fort Worth. Denton. What about you? Have you always been in the military?"

He nodded. "All of my life, and we moved around a lot. Dad was career air force, so I went into the academy after high school. I always wanted to fly."

She motioned toward his leg. "Is that how you were injured?"

He hated to think about that day. "Yeah, I had to eject from my aircraft and my landing wasn't the best."

"Well, it looks like you're on the mend."

He stiffened. "It's taking too long. I want to get back in the air."

Lindsey had heard some of the history of the Randell family, but Brady was a surprise to her. There was actually a Randell who wasn't a rancher. "So you're going back?"

"Why shouldn't I? I'm one of the best."

"And so humble, too." She forced a smile. "I'm sure the doctors are doing everything possible. Are you?"

His eyes narrowed. "What does that mean? Of course I'm doing everything, and that includes a lot of rigorous physical therapy."

"That's good." *Just keep your mouth shut, Lindsey*, she told herself as she looked around. *Where is Tess?*

"You don't like me much," he said.

"I barely know you, Captain Randell." And she wasn't sure she wanted to.

"You should know that I'm very good at what I do. And I plan to continue flying for the air force for a long time." He set his injured leg on the floor. "Sitting around a ranch house isn't for me."

"You don't seem to have a choice right now. So maybe you should use this time to count your blessings that you survived your accident instead of taking your anger out on every unsuspecting person who happens to cross your path."

"How the hell do you know what I've gone through?"

Lindsey was going through her own personal pain, too. Her stepfather didn't have such a rosy future.

"You're right, I don't, but I know you're healthy, with a family who loves you, and all you're doing is complaining."

His stony look told her that she'd gone too far. "I should go," she said. "I'm sure someone will be here shortly."

She stood, but before she could get to the door it opened and a little girl came running in.

"Uncle Brady, Uncle Brady. Mommy said you fell down." The little blonde went running to the stoic man on the sofa. "Are you hurt?" she cried.

"No darlin', I'm fine. I just tripped over my big feet and bumped my head."

The girl's worried look didn't leave until her uncle showed her the damage. "See, it's just a little bump."

The child leaned down and kissed it. "There, that will make it better."

Then it happened. Brady Randell sat back and a big smile appeared across the handsome face. Lindsey's heart leaped and she tried hard to remember the man with the bad attitude.

The little girl turned to her and smiled. "Mommy said you're Whiskey's new vet. I'm Livy Meyers Randell. My new daddy married my mommy and 'dopted me."

Lindsey smiled. "Well, it's nice to meet you, Livy Meyers Randell. I'm Lindsey Stafford."

"Hi, Miss Lindsey." A smile beamed on her cute face. "Thank you for taking care of Whiskey, and Uncle Brady."

"You're very welcome."

The child put her arm around her uncle's neck. "Did you know I'm gonna marry Uncle Brady when I grow up?"

You can have him, Lindsey thought. "Isn't that nice."

Lindsey hadn't planned to be gone all day, but she also hadn't planned to babysit an injured fighter pilot, either. That was until she'd been pushed aside by a five-year-old girl. It didn't matter her age, that female had already staked her claim on the man. What had amazed Lindsey was how Brady Randell's whole demeanor had changed when the child walked into the room.

She smiled. So he wasn't the tough guy he pretended to be.

Tired, Lindsey walked into the cabin the Randells had given her to use during her three-month stay. The one-bedroom structure was located in the Mustang

Valley Nature Retreat. This cabin had been designed as a romantic getaway.

A big, river-rock fireplace, plush rug and overstuffed love seat were the centerpieces of the main room. The bedroom consisted of a large four-poster bed with satin sheets and an abundance of candles. It connected to a bathroom with a whirlpool tub that easily held two.

Definitely for a couple.

It was off season, so she had the place to herself except for the herd of wild mustangs that roamed freely in this area.

The only drawback was she had to park her SUV at the top of the rise and walk or ride down in a golf cart. There were no vehicles allowed in this area.

Hank Barrett, the patriarch of the Randell family, was adamant about keeping his wild ponies protected. Lindsey felt the same way. So many people thought of them as nuisances, but the Randells had made sure this area was going to be left untouched.

No development in this valley. Ever.

Luke Randell was the project manager for a gated horse community being built on the land that edged the valley. But the project had many strict rules.

It was dusk, and Lindsey looked out the picture window at the scene below. Picking up the binoculars off the sill, she focused in on the grassy meadow. She sighed at seeing the half-dozen mustang ponies grazing peacefully.

Her chest constricted at the incredible sight. How could Jack Randell ever have left this place? More importantly, after all these years, how could she get him to come here? Back to his home…his boys.

CHAPTER TWO

THE following week Brady got some good news. At his doctor's visit the day before, he learned his fracture was healing well. Well enough that the bulkier cast had been replaced with a walking cast, so he could finally put weight on his leg. That meant he could get rid of the crutches and use a cane. And start more-intense therapy.

Finally it was time to get back in shape so he could get back into the cockpit.

Brady had also succumbed to Luke's badgering and gone along as he toured the construction site. He cursed as the golf cart bounced over the uneven ground. He grabbed the frame as he nearly flew out of his seat. "Hey, do you think you could have missed a few potholes back there?"

Luke grinned as he continued to maneuver the vehicle along the ridge. "Just wanted to make sure you haven't fallen asleep."

"Not the way you drive." Brady zipped up his flight jacket to help ward off the morning chill. "Besides, I don't need any more injuries added to my list."

His brother gave him a sideways glance. "I might have to call on the pretty veterinarian to come by. Seems she's the only one who can handle you."

Brady tensed. Not one of his proudest moments. "I didn't need to be handled by anyone. I was fine then and I'm fine now." He hadn't seen the hot redhead since that day. Probably a good thing. If he let her, Lindsey Stafford could be a powerful distraction.

Luke stopped the cart, then he sat back with a sigh. "Now, is this a view or what?" He motioned with his hand. "What do you think?"

Brady looked through the grove of ancient oak trees that shaded part of the valley below. A creek flowed around the sturdy trunks and through high, golden meadow grass.

In the peaceful silence, Brady felt a calm come over him. "Not a bad view." His gaze went to the other side of the rise where a small cabin nestled on the hillside. Farther on was another log structure, and another nearly hidden from view. "Who lives up there?"

"That's the Mustang Valley Nature Retreat. It's part of our holdings, too. There are about a dozen cabins that are rented out through the summer months. Some of the construction staff is living there now. And also your Dr. Stafford."

Brady refused to take the bait. "Why? Can't she afford to rent her own place?"

"Since she's here temporarily, Hank offered her one of the cabins for her stay."

"How temporary?"

"Just until Doc Hillman is able to handle his practice again." Luke stole a glance at his brother. "Tess would love for Lindsey to stay on permanently. Maybe it's because she's a woman, but she likes how Lindsey seems to take extra time with Whiskey."

"I take it the stallion's leg is healed, since I saw Tess working him yesterday. Is he okay to compete?"

Luke nodded. "We're headed to Fort Worth this next weekend. Tess is entering Whiskey in the nonpro NCHA Futurity. But don't worry, Bernice will be here if you need anything."

Brady hated everyone hovering over him. "I've managed to take care of myself most of my life, and I can handle it now."

Luke glanced down at Brady's new cast. "Seems you can get around better, too. How is the leg? Giving you any trouble since you've been walking on it?"

Sometimes it hurt like hell. "No. Between Dr. Pahl and the therapist conferring, I haven't been allowed to do much. But I get to start real therapy next week." His therapist, Brenna, was Dylan's wife, another cousin. She hadn't been easy on him so far, but he liked that about her. She'd warned him about starting out slow. He wasn't good at slow. He needed to get back into shape again, and fast. Granted, the wide-open beauty of Mustang Valley was peaceful, but he needed the vast sky through the cockpit of his F-16 to feed his soul.

"Is everyone around here related to us?" Brady asked.

Luke leaned back. "Just about. It takes getting used to, having all this family."

If he and Brady had anything in common, it was that they were both only children. "Being in the military, we moved around a lot. I didn't have a chance to make friends, so most of the time it was just the three of us."

"You had plenty of family—Uncle Jack's family—our dad just chose not to come back here."

Brady knew that he and Luke would never agree about Sam Randell. He'd abandoned his oldest son, but in truth, he wasn't around much to be a father to his second boy, either.

"So Dad chose a military career over ranching. I bet that didn't make a lot of people happy," Brady said.

"And he chose your mother over mine."

And me over you, Brady thought as his anger started to build. In truth, Sam had chosen his career over everyone. "Look, Luke, I thought you and I were okay with this. Whatever happened between our parents didn't have anything to do with us."

Luke stared out into the valley. "I'm okay with you, and our partnership. It's still hard sometimes." He let go of a long breath. "But like Tess said, I'm back home now." He turned to Brady. "And I finally got to meet my brother."

Brady wasn't about to get all mushy over the reunion. "And about a million cousins. Man, is there something about this valley that causes all these kids?"

Luke arched an eyebrow. "You got something against kids?"

"I don't mind one or two, but a squadron is a bit much."

Luke laughed. "I thought the same thing when I first came here. But they're all great kids, and our cousins are good parents. I believe it's because of their foster parent, Hank Barrett, who was a big influence on them. A lot more so than Jack Randell."

Brady smiled. "Oh, yeah, our uncle, the famous cattle rustler."

They both remained silent, reflecting on the past, when they spotted two riders. Brady recognized Tess on Lady and beside her another woman. A redhead with a familiar black hat.

"Looks like we have company." Luke leaned forward. "My Tess and your favorite doctor."

Brady groaned, but he found his pulse racing as he watched the two approach. Luke got out of the cart and went to his wife as she jumped down from her horse. Tess smiled at her husband, but when Brady turned his attention to Lindsey, she didn't show him any kind of special feminine greeting.

Good. He wasn't going to be here long enough to get tangled up with a woman. She wasn't his type, anyway. But as the redhead started toward him in her form-fitting jeans, cream-colored sweater and black nylon vest, his body suddenly called him a liar.

"Good morning, Mr. Randell."

Okay, he liked her a little, especially her attitude. "Since you've had your hands all over my body, don't you think you could call me Brady?"

She stopped next to the golf cart. "And since you're not that familiar with mine, you may call me Dr. Stafford."

He arched an eyebrow, letting his gaze speak for him. "The day isn't over yet."

She finally smiled. "How about Lindsey?"

"Oh, I don't know, I'm kind of leaning toward sexy doc."

She frowned. "Only if you want me to hurt you."

He glanced toward his brother and sister-in-law to see they were out of earshot. "When it comes to a beautiful woman, the last thing I'm thinking about is pain." He climbed out of the cart and stood in front of her. "I'm more a pleasure kind of guy."

Lindsey didn't like Brady Randell so close, but she refused to back away. "How about we stop the innuendos and try to have a normal conversation?"

He nodded. "Nice weather for a ride."

"Yes it is," she told him. "Tess invited me to go along to help thin the mustang herd and check for injuries. We're going to meet up with Hank Barrett and some of your cousins."

"So you're going to play doc?"

"I don't *play* doctor."

He raised a hand. "I only meant I wish I could go along and see you in action. But all I'm traveling in these days is this cart."

Lindsey knew the confinement had to be hard for Brady. She glanced down at the new, smaller cast. "It looks like you're making progress and will be back in the cockpit soon."

"That's what I'm shooting for."

She could see the cocky determination on his face. No doubt he looked even more handsome in his flight jumpsuit. She glanced down at his worn jeans, then upward to his straw Stetson. He wasn't a bad imitation of a cowboy, either.

"Maybe if your doctor approves, you could go out for a short ride. Nothing strenuous, of course. But I bet Tess has a gentle mount."

"I'd take anything at this point."

"Can you drive a car, yet?"

He nodded. "Since it's my left foot, yes, but only if

it's an automatic. My '67 Chevy Camaro back at the base is a stick shift."

She never doubted that for a second, or the fact that the vehicle was a hotrod. Brady Randell was definitely not her type. She was all about settling down, safety and animals. He was a death-defying jet jockey with no intention of letting grass grow under his boots. She looked up into his piercing eyes and her heart went crazy. Okay, speaking from a sensual aspect, this man was any woman's type.

She really needed to stay clear of him.

"I should get going. I have appointments this afternoon." She turned to find Tess lost in her husband's arms. They were exchanging kisses and whispered lover's secrets. The couple seemed unaware anyone else was around.

Brady came up behind her. "Those two are like that all the time. I hate to say it, but it makes me a little jealous."

Lindsey felt Brady's breath against her ear. The warmth of his large body shielded her from the cool morning. She closed her eyes momentarily. Yes, she longed to be part of a couple. To find the right man. Someday.

Right now she had other things to think about. Top on her list was the true reason she'd come to San Angelo, and her time was limited to find the answers she needed. Getting involved with a man would only complicate matters. She finally moved away from temptation.

"Tess," she called. "We need to get going if we're to meet up with Hank and the others." She glanced at Brady. "I'm glad you're doing well."

He leaned against his cane. "Like I said, I wish I was going with you, Doc."

"Maybe when your leg is healed," she promised as she backed away. Was she crazy?

"I'll look forward to it," he called. "I'll work to make sure it's soon."

Lindsey was still chiding herself when they reached the edge of the valley. There was high grass mixed in with thick native mesquite bushes. Ancient oak trees arched over the riding path like a canopy filtering the sunlight. The November day was brisk, causing her skin to tingle. She felt exhilarated.

Her thoughts returned to Brady. She hadn't expected to see him again so soon. He'd looked considerably better than the last time. He'd shaved and was dressed in jeans and a gray U.S. Air Force sweatshirt under his bomber jacket. In a cowboy hat, he looked cocky and sure of himself.

"How are you holding up?" Tess asked as she rode up beside her.

"I'm fine. In fact if I could schedule it, I'd ride every day."

Tess smiled. "I come out to check the ponies every week during the winter. I could saddle up Dusty and bring him by the cabin for you."

"If I'm not busy, I'd love it." She patted the seasoned buckskin gelding, remembering her childhood days at the ranch. She loved the freedom of riding. It had been her escape from a lot of problems, especially during her parents' abusive marriage. "You sure you don't mind me borrowing Dusty?"

"Anytime. Since Dad can't ride anymore, I appreciate anyone who exercises him."

Lindsey's heart softened. Tess's father was in the beginning stages of Alzheimer's. "Good. I'll let you know my schedule."

"And maybe you can help get Brady up and riding, too."

Lindsey glanced over to see Tess's smile. "Shouldn't he walk before he gets on a horse?"

Tess shrugged. "Maybe he can do both. We're willing to try anything to get him out of the house. Luke managed today, but not without a lot of prodding."

She couldn't imagine the captain doing anything he didn't want to do. "It's a start."

"Since the two had never met until a few months ago, both Luke and Brady are still getting to know each other. If their father, Sam Randell, hadn't left them both the ranch, I wonder if they would have ever met."

"Then it's good they have this opportunity."

"I feel the same way," Tess said. "Although they do have very different views of their father. Luke was deserted by Sam when his parents divorced. Brady had him around most of his life."

Lindsey rested her hands on the saddle horn, letting Dusty take the lead. "Sometimes there isn't a choice."

"There's always a choice," Tess murmured, then pointed up ahead. "There's Hank, Cade and Chance."

Lindsey knew Hank Barrett was the one who'd taken in the three Randell brothers, Chance, Cade and Travis, to raise after their father, Jack, had been sent to prison.

As they got closer to the men on horseback, Lindsey could see the strong family resemblance between the brothers. It seemed all Randell men were tall, with that rangy, muscular build. The square jaw and cleft in the chin was like a brand, telling the world who they belonged to.

She'd met Chance and Travis earlier, but Cade looked even more like the man Lindsey had called Dad for the past fifteen years.

The difference was these men shared his blood. She didn't.

Jack Randell was only her stepfather.

Just as soon as Jack and her mother returned home from their vacation and discovered she'd gone against his wishes, he wouldn't be happy.

It wasn't as though she'd planned to come to San Angelo. It had been curiosity that had her go to the job interview. She told herself she only wanted to meet Travis, one of Jack's sons. Then she found herself accepting the position. After all, it was only temporary.

Hank Barrett sat back in the saddle and watched Tess approach with the new veterinarian. Ever since Travis returned from Dallas singing Dr. Lindsey Stafford's praises, Hank had been anxious to meet her.

He smiled as the redhead rode closer. She was easy on the eyes, and if there was one thing he appreciated, it was a pretty female, no matter what the age.

Hank greeted Tess. "Hello, Mrs. Randell."

"Good morning, Mr. Barrett," she answered. "Hi, Cade, Chance."

Chance touched the brim of his hat in greeting. "Tess." He glanced at the redhead. "Dr. Stafford, nice seeing you again. This is our other brother, Cade.

And this is Hank Barrett, the one who started the mustang project."

Hank nodded at the petite woman who sat comfortably in the saddle. There was something about her name that was familiar. "Dr. Stafford, I'm glad you could join us.

"Please, everyone, call me Lindsey." Her horse shifted sideways. "And thank you for inviting me along today."

"Well, Lindsey," Hank began, "I hope you still feel that way if the ponies don't cooperate. They've been known to be stubborn."

The doctor rewarded him with a smile. "I hear old Dusty here is pretty good at cutting out his target."

Cade reined his roan back. "I guess we'll know soon enough if he likes to chase wild ponies as much as cows." He grinned and Lindsey tensed, once again seeing the resemblance to his father.

"I'd say we better get going," Chance said, pointing to the herd off in the distance.

Lindsey looked at Hank for direction as they started down the trail.

"We'll let Chance and Cade take the lead," he said. "Wyatt, Dylan and Jarred are at the other end of the canyon to drive the herd toward us."

"I'll just follow you," she said.

Hank nodded. "Okay, let's go and get us some ponies."

They rode off, and Lindsey felt she was taking a step back in time. To see the wild ponies in their natural setting. This had been another big draw for her to come here. She just didn't realize how much she would already love it.

Two hours later Brady sat with Luke in his truck, waiting at the temporary corral at Hank's ranch, the

Circle B Ranch. He was still wondering why he'd come. Of course, it beat the alternative, sitting back at the cottage. That had been what he told Luke, anyway. Not that he wanted another chance to see Lindsey Stafford again.

"They're coming," Luke called as he climbed down off the railing.

His own excitement growing, Brady got out of the truck and looked to where his brother pointed. He saw the riders on horseback, chasing after the ponies. An assorted mixture of paints, bays and buckskins. Over a dozen as far as he could see. But he couldn't find Lindsey.

"There's Tess," Luke called.

It was easy to catch his sister-in-law's long blond hair. Then he spotted Lindsey's black hat. She was riding drag, a bandana tied around the lower part of her face to help filter the dust.

"Come on, bro, help me with the gates." Brady was glad he could finally manage to do something useful. He followed his brother, took one side and swung open the metal gate. It had been a while since he'd been around horses, but he knew they could be unpredictable at best. The first two ponies arrived and went into the pen, but the third and fourth decided to turn off.

Hanging on to the gate, Brady yanked off his hat, waved it around and yelled to turn the horse back. Then Chance and Cade showed up to take over. Finally the last of the ponies were in the large pen and the gate shut.

His cousins climbed off their horses and everyone went to the corral to check out their finds. Brady's gaze was on Lindsey. She dismounted and walked toward the metal railing with the old guy, Hank.

Barrett looked the part of mentor, father and grandfather. He didn't have to demand respect, but he got it. He wasn't a Randell, but he'd earned the title of family patriarch.

He nodded at Brady. "Good to see you up and around."

"It's a start."

"Well, if you get the doctor's okay, you can go out with us the next time."

Brady nodded. Chances were, if he was strong enough to chase wild mustangs, he'd be hightailing it for the cockpit of his F-16. "Thank you, sir," Brady said. "I'd like that."

Hank turned back to Lindsey. "I think we got ourselves a good-looking bunch this time."

Lindsey avoided Brady's gaze and went up to the gate. "I'm worried about the paint. See how he favors the right front leg?"

Brady looked, too, but he had to watch closely to see the slight limp.

"It could be a pebble. I'm going to have to examine him, but I have appointments this afternoon."

Hank agreed as he checked his watch. "Tomorrow, then. We'll separate them so they all can be examined and inoculated. How's that with you, Doc?"

"I could come by tomorrow afternoon for a few hours."

"Good, it will give us time to see which ponies are worth the time to saddle break."

"Why are you saddle breaking them?" Brady asked.

"So we can sell them at auction. Since we have to thin the herd, we want to find good homes for them."

Brady had his eye on a gray stallion that didn't like being confined in the pen. He kept moving back and forth along the fence.

Hank waved the group on. "Everyone is welcome to come up to the house for lunch. Lindsey, I hope you can join us."

"I'd like that." She pulled out her phone. "I just need to check my messages." She hung back from the group.

Hank looked at Brady. "How about you, Captain? I wouldn't mind hearing a few F-16 stories."

"I might have one or two that are worth repeating." Using his cane, Brady managed to fall into step beside Hank. Although his steps were awkward, he was happy to be able to get around. What he couldn't understand was why he was feeling drawn to this family. Not to mention one vet.

They made their way into the compound where a large ranch house stood. It was painted glossy white with dark green trim. The barn and other buildings were also white and well kept.

"Nice place, Hank," Brady said.

"Thanks. My boys run things now. In the summer months we open it as a dude ranch of sorts, but it's a working ranch." He grinned. "You'd be surprised what people will pay just to do chores like a ranch hand."

Cade joined the group. "Yeah, Chance, Travis and I had to do the work for nothing growing up."

"It built character," Hank told him.

Cade laughed. "Well, I sure got a lot of that, then."

Brady listened to the teasing between the brothers and Hank. Suddenly he thought back to how much his own father had been away during his life. All the baseball games he'd missed, the birthdays and holidays. As a typical kid he did a lot to get Sam's attention. Most of it didn't work, until he got into ROTC in high school, then into the academy.

"You boys turned out okay," Hank said. "You've settled down with pretty wives and have families."

Brady glanced over his shoulder and caught sight of Lindsey hurrying to catch up, so he hung back.

"Do you have to run off?"

"No, I can stay for lunch. But I have a two-o'clock appointment."

"Good, that will give me time," he said.

She frowned. "Time for what?"

"Time to convince you I'm not a total jerk."

"Really." She looked skeptical. "You think I should go easy on you?"

"No, but I'm hoping my Randell charm will win out."

She smiled. "So the average guy doesn't have a chance over a Randell?"

"That's right."

They took slow, easy steps toward the back porch.

"Well, I disagree on that theory," she said. "Jarred Trager, and Dylan and Wyatt Gentry do all right in the charm department."

Brady fought rising jealousy, recalling how his cousins had been flirting with her earlier. They had their own wives. "That just goes to show you a Randell wins out."

She stopped and looked confused. "But they're not Randells?"

He nodded. "Yes, they are. Seems Uncle Jack had three more sons."

CHAPTER THREE

AS HARD AS LINDSEY TRIED, she couldn't hide her shock. "Really" was all she could come up with.

Brady gave a sharp nod. "Evidently Uncle Jack was quite the lady's man when he was out on the rodeo circuit."

"Have Jarred, Wyatt and Dylan always lived here?"

Brady shook his head. "About half a dozen years ago, Jarred Trager showed up. He had found an old letter from Jack to his mother that talked about their affair. He came here and met Dana Shayne and her son, Evan. They married a short time later." He shrugged. "That's the condensed version that Luke gave me."

Lindsey took easy breaths as they continued on toward the Barrett house. She walked slowly so Brady could keep up, and so she could try to absorb what he told her. Had Jack known about his other sons?

"You say Wyatt and Dylan are your cousins, too?" She should have seen the resemblance in the men.

He nodded. "After their mother finally told the twins who their father was, Wyatt came to San Angelo looking for Jack, too. Wyatt ended up buying Uncle Jack's half of the Rocking R and found Maura Wells and her two kids, Jeff and Holly, living in the rundown house. A few months later his twin, Dylan, arrived after he'd been injured bull riding. He ended up marrying his physical therapist, Brenna. Who, by the way, is putting me through torture these days."

They reached the porch and he turned to her. "You seem pretty curious about the Randell family."

She shrugged. "The Randells are a big part of this valley. As an only child it's interesting to hear about a large family."

"Yeah, aren't we just one, big happy family."

"I'd take them," Lindsey told him, trying to act lighthearted. It was difficult. From the beginning, Jack had warned her and her mother about his shady past. She also realized that her stepfather needed to know about his other sons. If only to make amends with them.

Suddenly the back door opened and Hank peered out. "There you are. I was wondering if you two had gotten lost."

Brady used the railing to climb the steps. "No, I'm a little slow these days."

Hank smiled. "I thought you were just hanging back to get some time with a pretty lady."

"Well, that, too."

Lindsey felt her heart accelerate, but she put on a smile. "Well, now that we're here, how about some lunch?"

Hank ushered them into a huge old fashioned kitchen. Sunny yellow walls were lined with maple cupboards. The white-tiled counter gleamed, and a tall, older woman was busy setting the table.

She turned and smiled. "Hello, you must be the new vet, Dr. Stafford. I'm Hank's wife, Ella."

"And I'm Lindsey."

Her friendly brown eyes searched Lindsey's face. "It's nice to meet you. Hank said you were pretty, and he's right."

Cade walked by her. "Hank says all the women are pretty."

"That's because all the women around here *are* pretty." Hank hugged his wife to his side, kissing her cheek.

Ella acted as if she were pushing him away. "Be careful, Lindsey. Hank will be wanting to know if you're a good cook, too."

Hank tried to look indignant. "I hardly know this woman. But if she can cook up any special dishes, I wouldn't mind sampling them, say at our next family get-together. Thanksgiving is coming up."

Cade grinned as he took his seat at the table. "Watch what you say, Hank, or Ella will have you sleeping in the bunkhouse."

The group hooted with laughter, and Lindsey quickly realized she'd been had. "Well, sorry to disappoint you, Hank, but I spent all my free time studying the last few years. So my culinary skills are sorely lacking."

Hank sighed. "That's going to make it harder for you to get a man."

Lindsey was too stunned to speak, but Tess did it for her. "Hank Barrett, stop your teasing. We want Lindsey to stay, not run her off." She turned to Lindsey. "Please sit down, unless you want to clobber Hank first."

Lindsey walked around the table. "I think I'll wait until I have some big instruments in my hand."

The table broke into another round of laughter as she

took a seat next to Tess and Luke. Brady managed to snag the seat next to hers.

He leaned toward her and murmured, "You sure know how to hold your own, Doc. I should call you when I'm being chewed out by my commanding officer."

"I can't imagine that ever happening, not with your sweet disposition."

Those dark bedroom eyes bore into hers. "I'm workin' on changing that." He grinned. "Give me a little time, and my charm will melt you."

Lindsey knew Brady was more dangerous than any of the Randells. Because he was the one who could get to her. And when he discovered who she was, he wouldn't be happy. None of the Randells would be, not when they learned that Jack had hung around to play the doting father to her.

Brady hated being cooped up. That was the reason three mornings later he headed down to the barn. He needed the exercise. He'd been lifting weights to keep in shape, but hanging around the cottage was driving him up a wall.

He told himself it wasn't the possibility of meeting up with Lindsey and Tess coming back from their ride. It was just to take a walk. He ran into the groomer washing Lady and ended up helping with some of the light chores. He found that working his muscles felt good. Just being able to complete a simple task helped his mood. By the time an hour was up, the temperature had warmed. He'd shed his jacket and was mucking out a stall when Tess and Lindsey came into the barn.

Both women were laughing, their cheeks flushed

from the cool weather as they led their horses. Lindsey spotted him, and her smile dropped.

Tess spoke first. "Brady, what are you doing out here?"

"Earning my keep," he told his sister-in-law. "It's about time I did something around here."

Tess glanced down at the cast on his foot. "Just so long as you don't do any damage."

"I've been careful, *Mom*," he teased.

Tess fought a smile and lost. "Well, you can go out and play." She turned to Lindsey. "I hate to run off, but I need to meet Livy's bus. Juan can handle the horses until I get back."

"Not a problem, I can stay and take care of my horse," Lindsey said as she took the reins from her. "It's the least I can do for you letting me ride. So go on, go get your daughter."

"Thanks." Tess smiled as she backed away.

"I can help, too," Brady said.

"There's no need," Lindsey said. "I would hate to take you away from your job."

Brady didn't back away. "Then after I help you, you can help me. There are two more stalls to clean. Unless it's too dirty a job for you."

She made an unladylike snort. "I've probably mucked out more stalls than you've seen. I grew up on a horse ranch."

He took Whiskey's reins from her. He loved to see her get riled. It made her eyes turn a deep emerald green. "You probably have. We didn't live very long on our ranch."

They walked slowly to the stallion's stall. Right next to it was Dusty's. "Where was your ranch?" she asked.

"We had a small place in Utah not far from the base. Dad bought it with his reenlistment bonus. With the help of a foreman, he ran a small yearling operation for about four years. I was ten when he was sent overseas and had to sell the place." He wasn't sure why he was telling her this. He tossed the stirrup over the seat and unfastened the cinch, then pulled the saddle off the horse and took it to the stand outside the stall. After Lindsey pulled off Dusty's, he took it. He liked moving around, being active. He found his balance was a lot better.

"Thanks." She went to work on the rest of the tack. "It's a shame you never got to live here."

"Dad never told me about the Rocking R until last year when he got sick."

"Had he been ill for long?"

Brady shrugged, remembering the hulk of a man who had slowly faded away after he retired from the air force. Even his wife, Georgia, hadn't been enough to keep him happy and at home. She'd died alone.

"Dad ignored the doctor's advice," he told her. "After he retired, I don't think he cared much if he lived or died." He gaze met hers. "They say I'm a lot like him. All I've known is the military."

Lindsey paused at her task, hearing the sadness in his voice, seeing it in his eyes. She suspected coming here and meeting the Randells had been overwhelming for him.

She suddenly thought of Jack. What was going to happen to him, when he was too stubborn to help himself? Well, she couldn't let that happen, not without doing everything possible, at the very least to get him to see his sons.

"Are you okay?"

Hearing Brady's voice, Lindsey pushed away the wayward thoughts. "I'm fine. Just thinking about how lucky you are to find your brother," she said. "And to be able to come here, and be with family."

He snorted. "Hell, I knew nothing about all these cousins. Dad never talked about them. Most of the time, it was just Mom and me." He shrugged. "We moved around a lot. But, hey, I got to see the world before I was in high school."

"Too bad you never got to come here."

He straightened. "My dad had to go where the air force sent him. That's the way it was then, and the way it is now. You go where you're assigned."

Lindsey nodded. "I bet your dad was proud of you."

He blinked, as if the question caught him off guard. "Hell, I guess so. Why so many questions?"

She had no doubt this man didn't share much about himself. "I'm just curious."

"Okay, here's the lowdown. I'm a fighter pilot in the U.S. Air Force. I'm qualified to fly F-15 and F-16 and at this time stationed out of Hill AFB in Utah." He moved closer. "Do you want my rank and serial number?" He reached inside his shirt and pulled out his dog tags. The chain dangled in his hand as if to taunt her.

"No, I think I have enough info."

She returned to her task of removing the gelding's bridle, a little embarrassed. She didn't have any business questioning this man or thinking about developing any feelings for him.

"Family is important, Brady. Get to know your brother and cousins before the chance slips away."

"I don't seem to have a choice, for now, anyway." He

looked down at his injured leg. "There's no guarantee that I can go back to flying."

"Even if you can't fly again, there are other careers in the air force."

"Not for me." A muscle tightened in his jaw. "It's who I am. It's the only thing I've ever wanted to do."

"Flying can't define you as a person, Brady. It's what you love, yes, but not who you are. You can do something else, or go wherever. Maybe even live here."

"I hardly see myself as a rancher. I need a little more excitement." He relaxed as his dark-eyed gaze settled on her face. "Of course, if you'll be around…"

She was caught off guard. "My job here is temporary."

A slow, lazy grin appeared. No doubt a sample of the Randell killer charm. "Yeah, but you could make it permanent. Everyone wants you to stay on." His gaze moved over her. "And I could make a point to come back here for an occasional visit."

Lindsey refused to react to Brady's arrogant comment. She had other worries. For one, would she be welcome after they learned her real reason for being here? "You'd be wasting your time, Captain."

His dark eyes narrowed. "Why? Is there a man back in Fort Worth?"

She looked at him. "Yes, there is someone back home."

Brady hated being caught off guard, and he was truly blindsided by Lindsey Stafford. The only good thing was that Tess walked into the barn before she could tell him about her man.

He grabbed his cane and headed out the door. He didn't like the game Lindsey Stafford was playing. With women in the past, he set the rules. No attachments and no commitments. Have some fun, then walk away. So far there hadn't been any fun, but he sure as hell was doing the walking.

He should have known she'd be trouble the second he first saw her. He climbed the porch steps, went into the cottage and didn't stop until he got to the kitchen and pulled a can of iced tea from the refrigerator. After a long drink, he worked on calming down. He was going to erase her from his head. But he doubted anything would do the job.

What surprised him was why this even bothered him. She was leaving in a few months. So what? He was going back to his base in Utah. And besides there were other women…a lot of women.

A knock sounded on the door, but he ignored it. When the knocking continued he figured it was probably Luke or Tess. They wouldn't give up. He finally went and pulled open the door.

Damned if Lindsey wasn't standing there on his porch.

"Did you forget to tell me something else?"

She didn't act sorry. "Yes. Before you took off, I was about to mention that the man in my life—"

"Believe me," he interrupted, "I'm not interested."

She didn't move. "The man is my stepfather."

His heart began to race. "Your stepfather?"

"Yes. He's been ill recently, and I don't want to make any long commitments away from home."

Brady watched the sadness play on her face, and the sudden tightness in his gut caught him off guard. He reached for her and pulled her inside the house. Closing the door, he pushed her back against the wall.

"Do you know you had me crazy, thinking all sorts of things?"

She blinked as her breathing grew rapid. "You didn't let me tell you anything else," she whispered.

Her slim body was pressed against his, reminding him how long he'd been without a woman. "All I want to know is if you have someone special in your life, a husband, a significant other, a friend with benefits." He raised an eyebrow, praying she'd give him the right answer.

"No, none of the above."

Brady's resolve disappeared as he cupped her face and lowered his head to hers. "Maybe we should work on that," he breathed just as his mouth closed over hers.

She tasted sweet and sexy at the same time. He hungered for her like no woman before. He couldn't get enough of her as his tongue dove into her mouth. Lindsey murmured something deep in her throat and her arms slipped around his neck.

Brady slid his hands inside her coat, under her sweat-shirt to her bare back, and pulled her as close to him as possible. The imprint of her breasts against his chest nearly drove him over the edge.

He still needed more. His fingers traced across her warm, soft skin to her breasts. The material was thin enough to feel her pebbled nipples through the lace. This time he groaned.

With a gasp, he broke off the kiss and sucked air into his starved lungs. He tried to slow the drumming of his heart as his gaze searched hers to find the same need and raw desire.

"You shouldn't have done that," she breathed.

He shook his head. "Probably not, Doc. But my

common sense doesn't seem to be working right now," he assured her as his head lowered to hers again.

Lindsey had called herself every kind of fool by the time she made her way back to the cabin. She'd managed to escape Brady Randell's arms, but just barely.

Once inside she leaned back against the door and shut her eyes only to relive the man's mind-blowing kisses. The feel of his hands on her skin as his mouth expertly caressed hers turning her into a whimpering teenager. What in the world had possessed her to go after him? To soothe his ego? To poke at the lion in his den?

She could still see those dark eyes, and that sexy grin spread across his face, looking as if he'd just conquered Mt. Everest. Lindsey groaned. She didn't need this kind of distraction to add to the already complicated situation.

She hadn't come here to get involved with a man, especially a cocky jet pilot with an ego that needed to be stroked. Well, she wasn't stroking anything of Brady Randell's. He wasn't her type. She never could handle a casual affair, no matter how good-looking and tempting the man was.

It would be wise to keep her distance. She needed to focus her attention on Brady's cousins. Jack's sons.

Lindsey's thoughts turned to her stepfather and the phone conversation she'd overheard during her last visit home in September.

Ever since Jack's first leukemia diagnosis four years ago, she and her mother had kept a close watch on his health. She'd recalled her stepfather's year of intense chemotherapy. How they'd almost lost him. He pulled through, and had been in remission for nearly three years. Until this last checkup.

Jack didn't want to tell her, but he finally admitted what the doctor reported, that any chemotherapy treatment wouldn't help him. He needed a bone marrow transplant to survive. That was when Lindsey begged Jack to contact his sons. He refused adamantly, saying he'd done enough damage in their lives, he couldn't ask anything from them.

Then Jack made Lindsey swear she wouldn't tell her mother. He didn't want to ruin the long Panama Canal cruise they'd planned for months. He promised to tell her before they got back.

Lindsey reluctantly agreed, hoping she could help convince him to contact his sons. Then she saw the ad for a temporary veterinarian position in San Angelo and the referral name of Travis Randell. She had to go. If only to meet one of Jack's sons. One of the boys he'd abandoned when he was sent off to prison.

Suddenly her cell phone rang and she dug into her purse to find it. "Hello."

"Well, I was wandering if you'd ever answer your phone." Jack Randell's voice came through loud and clear.

She tried to calm her panic. "Dad, you're back?"

"Not quite, your mother and I are spending another week away. We're in Los Angeles visiting friends."

She sighed in relief. "That's great, you two haven't had a vacation in so long."

"How about you, Lindy? How's the job hunting going?"

"Oh, I've had a few interviews, but I'm still looking for just the right position." She'd already found it, but knew that she'd never be able to stay here.

She changed the subject. "Have you had a chance to tell Mom?"

There was a long hesitation. "The right time hasn't come up, yet."

She closed her eyes. "Oh, Dad. I wish you'd think about what I suggested."

"Look, Lin, your mother wants to talk to you, so I'll say goodbye for now. I love you."

Tears filled her eyes. "I love you, too, Dad."

"Lindsey?" her mother said when she got on the phone. "How are you, honey?"

"Outside of missing you guys, pretty good. The job hunting is slow." She lied again and hated it. She and her mom had gone through a lot together before Jack came into their lives. She didn't like keeping this secret from her.

"I think you should hold out for what you want. And you know Jack and I would love to have you close to home."

That was her problem. Lindsey had already felt as if she'd come home, right here. "I've got my résumé out there, but I might just have to take something temporary until the good job comes around. I still have school loans to pay back."

"You know we want to help you."

"Thanks, Mom. I'm fine."

"My independent daughter." She heard her mother giggle, knowing Jack was probably distracting her. "Maybe you should take some time off. Go on a vacation and find yourself a man."

Lindsey's thoughts turned to Brady. She already had, but she couldn't compete with his lifestyle. Captain Randell was definitely off-limits. For more reasons than she could count.

The next morning Lindsey was awakened by pounding on her door. "Just a minute," she called as she threw on a robe over her pajamas, walked out of the bedroom and across the tiled floor through the main room.

Who could be here this early?

She tossed her mussed hair back as she opened the door to find Brady on her porch. He was in jeans and his flight jacket and the usual straw cowboy hat.

"Brady?"

"Morning, Doc." He walked inside with a sight limp.

"Uh, it's a little early to visit don't you think?" She glanced at the clock over the fireplace that read 6:30 a.m. and hugged her robe together.

He smiled. "This is the best part of the day. I loved those early-morning runs, the sun just coming up over the horizon." He released a breath. "Nothing like it, being all alone with the endless sky overhead and the desert floor below." Then he came out of his thoughts. "Or if I'm in a roll, the sky below and the ground above."

She watched the flicker of emotions play over his face and it tugged at her heart. "You miss it, don't you?"

He shrugged. "There's no rush like it." Then he straightened. "I'm sorry to bother you, but I was taking a ride in the golf cart this morning. That's when I saw the mustang. A mare. She's either lame or hurt."

Lindsey was on her way outside before Brady

finished explaining. The cold weather had her hugging her robe together. "Where? Is she close by?"

Brady looked out. "She was. It's that little buckskin. Maybe she just picked up a rock."

"Or maybe worse. Hank told me he had some trouble a few months back when one of the mustangs was wounded. He said it looked like someone was shooting pellets."

"You think we should call Hank?" he asked.

"I'll have a look first."

"I'm going with you."

She didn't need to be anywhere around this man. But he could help her find the pony. She looked down at her pajamas. "Give me five minutes."

The golf cart wasn't easy to maneuver over the rough terrain, but it was all they had at the moment. A few hundred yards away Brady spotted the small herd of mustangs. Hanging back from the others was the mare.

So as not to disturb them, he drove the cart along the edge of the trees. "That's her," he said, his voice soft and even.

Stopping, he handed the binoculars to Lindsey. As she adjusted the focus to watch the herd, Brady couldn't help but watch her. She was pretty, though not in the traditional way. Her eyes were too large for her face, and very expressive. Her mouth was full, those lips… He swallowed, recalling her taste. She sure got his attention.

When she'd opened the door this morning, he'd lost all conscious thought as to why he was there. Her hair wild, her eyes with that sleepy quality, her mouth looking so kissable. Like yesterday, he found it hard to resist her and wanted nothing more than to carry her back to where she came from. Bed.

"Bingo," Lindsey said, still watching the mare. "I can spot a smear of blood high on her right forearm."

"How bad?" He took the binoculars from her and looked for himself.

"Bad enough that the wound should be treated." She got out of the cart and reached in the backseat for her bag. "I wonder if she'll let me get close to her."

"No need. I'll get her." Brady got out, went to the back of the cart, pulled up the seat and took a rope from the compartment.

She came after him. "You can't. Let me help."

He glared at her. "If I need your help I'll holler."

Lindsey had no doubt Brady could do this with or without a bad leg, or he'd die trying. And she had to let him.

"Fine." She went back to her seat.

For a big man, he moved quietly and swiftly in his athletic shoes, even with his walking cast. Most men would look clumsy. But not Brady.

After tying the end of the rope to a tree, he walked carefully behind the herd. One of the stallions whinnied and danced away, putting more distance between them. The mare looked up and began to shy away.

"It's okay, princess," Brady said, keeping his voice quiet and even. "I'm not going to hurt you, girl. I just want to help make you feel better."

The mare bobbed her head, but didn't move away from the intruder. Unlike the rest of the herd that had wandered farther down the meadow. Brady continued his journey as he crooned to the trembling buckskin. Surprisingly, he handled the rope expertly making the large loop. Mesmerized by his husky voice, Lindsey barely noticed when he slipped the lasso around the mare's neck, then led her back to the cart.

The docile pony followed without much resistance. Lindsey knew from Tess that the mare had been around for a long time. And by the look of the blood on her forearm, she was wounded.

"I guess my persistence as a kid learning to rope a steer paid off," he remarked as he held the mare steady.

"Hello, girl," Lindsey said softly. She moved slowly so she wouldn't spook the horse.

Brady shortened the rope so the animal couldn't move. "Come on, princess, Doc only wants to help you."

Lindsey tried to get a look, but the mare wouldn't let her too close. There was no doubt that there was blood and she saw the fresh entry wound of a bullet.

Lindsey stood. "She's been shot."

"Damn." Brady looked around. "Guess I should call Hank." He pulled out his phone. "He isn't going to be happy to learn someone's invaded Mustang Valley."

CHAPTER FOUR

IT TOOK nearly thirty minutes for Lindsey and Brady to lead the mustang to the Circle B Ranch. They could have transported her to the clinic, but Lindsey didn't want to take the time or traumatize the mare any more than necessary.

Lindsey had to anesthetize the animal to remove the .22 bullet embedded in the fleshy part of her forearm. The surgery went well, thanks to the help of Hank and Brady.

She went into Hank's house to clean up, then she returned to the barn to check the patient. The pony would be groggy from the anesthesia, and Lindsey wanted to keep a close watch on her for the next few days before they released her back out to the range.

When she entered the cool interior of the barn she paused at the sight of Brady leaning over the pony's stall, his injured leg rested on the lowest rail. Her attention went to his worn jeans pulled taut over his nicely shaped butt. She couldn't help but take the time to admire the view.

"How's my girl doing?" Brady crooned. Not surprisingly the little mare reacted to his voice. He didn't attempt to touch her, but waited until she came to him. She did, but only so close.

"Don't be afraid, sweetheart. I'm not gonna hurt you."

Lindsey closed her eyes as his deep voice reverberated through her. She didn't doubt that Captain Randell had spoken those words many times. To how many women? She also knew she couldn't be added to that list, but it was getting harder and harder to convince herself. Not even when she knew if she gave in it would be disastrous.

Suddenly Brady glanced over his shoulder, those dark eyes alert as he examined her closely. "Hi."

"Hi." She nodded toward the horse. "Looks like you've made a friend."

"What can I say? Females can't resist me."

She couldn't help but laugh. "And modest, too."

He walked toward her. "Haven't you heard? Viper pilots are a cocky bunch."

"How does that combination work for you?"

He shrugged. "Not bad." He leaned his forearms against the railing, his gaze zoned in on hers. "What works on you, Doc?"

Her heart pounded in her chest as she tried to come up with a believable lie. "I'm not interested in a fling, Captain. I'm too busy for one thing, and smart enough not to start something with a man who will be leaving soon."

He frowned. "You must know more than I do."

"Come on, Brady, we both know our careers come first. You're going to work like crazy to get back to flying your F-16, and I'm going to work just as hard to get my practice off the ground."

He took off his hat and ran his fingers through his short hair. "That doesn't mean we can't enjoy time with each other."

That would be a bad idea, she thought. "In the biblical sense, of course."

He gave her the once-over. "We don't have to jump into anything, but that could be…interesting."

"And like I said, that's dangerous."

"I would go for incredible. I seem to remember a kiss yesterday that nearly blew my socks off."

Hers, too. "So we just go for instant gratification?"

He shrugged. "Would it be so bad?"

She glared at him.

"Okay, okay. Then, how about we go for friends? You're just about the only person around here who isn't a Randell or related to one."

She tensed. Okay, technically she wasn't a Randell. But when her identity was discovered, Brady's loyalty would go to his family. That was the best reason she needed to put a stop to this. And now.

From the doorway of the barn, Hank watched Brady and Lindsey. Anyone who had any horse sense could see there was something brewing between those two.

The brooding captain's whole demeanor had changed since the pretty vet had shown up in town. Now, if they could just find a way to get Lindsey to give him a chance, then maybe they'd both stick around. Old Doc Hillman wanted to retire, or at least bring in another vet as a partner in the practice, and Lindsey Stafford would be perfect.

Stafford. He wished he could remember why that name sounded familiar.

"Hank?"

He turned around to see Ella. A rush of feelings stirred in him as he smiled at his wife.

"Is there trouble with the mare?"

"No, she seems to be coming along fine. I was just enjoying the scene." He nodded at the couple. "Mark my word, there's sparks between those two."

"Of course there is. They're young, good-looking and their hormones are on a rampage."

Ella had been the best thing that had happened to him in a long time. He'd been a fool to have taken years to realize his love for her. He drew her close to his side. "You don't have to be young to have those feelings."

She actually blushed and pushed him away. "Hank Barrett, stop talking like that. Someone might hear."

"So what if they do? We're not dead, woman. So don't put me out to pasture just yet." He took her hand. "Now, come on, let's go see how the mare is doing."

Hank and Ella reached the stall. "How she doin'?" he asked.

"She's coming along fine," Lindsey said. "But you should keep her a day or two longer. I'll give her another dose of antibiotics in the morning." She raised an eyebrow. "Did you report the shooting?"

Hank nodded. "Called the sheriff, but I'm sorry to say that it isn't a top priority. A lot of people don't care for the wild horses. That's the reason I wanted to make sure this land was a haven for them. I thought it would keep them safe." He turned to the pretty vet. "I appreciate all that you've done, Lindsey."

"I'm just glad Brady found the mare in time."

Brady shrugged. "I got lucky."

Hank grew serious. "Lucky or not, we appreciate it, Brady. Thank you, too. And you can bet I'm going to take the threat to heart. This has happened before and it's time I put a stop to it. I won't allow someone to trespass on my land and endanger my stock, or worse, my family."

Hank sighed. "And since the sheriff won't do much, I'm going to have to go out myself and find these good-for-nothin' cowards. Even if it's some crazy kids, we still have to stop them."

"I'd like to go along," Brady said.

Hank knew the captain had a lot to prove, mostly to himself. "And I welcome your help, son, but I don't want any heroics here."

Brady nodded. "You give the orders."

"I thought we'd do some investigating. Maybe the person or persons left behind some clues."

"I can help, too," Lindsey volunteered.

Hank wasn't sure about that. "I was thinking about sending the boys out on horseback. And we might not get back until after dark."

"I've ridden after dark," she added.

"Maybe it would be safer if you went by truck with Brady. You two seem to make a good team."

By late afternoon Lindsey was exhausted when she entered the cabin. After leaving the Circle B, she'd finished her scheduled appointments, and now only had twenty minutes before Brady was due to pick her up. Although she was eager to help, she had plenty of apprehension over being paired with the one man she'd been trying to avoid. But she cared enough about the mustangs to want to find the person or persons who were responsible for the shooting.

After a quick shower, Lindsey hurriedly dressed in clean jeans and a sweatshirt over a thermal T-shirt and slipped on her comfortable boots. She slapped together two ham sandwiches and was just finishing up when a knock sounded on the door. She opened it to find Brady. He, too, was dressed in a sweatshirt, jeans and his bomber jacket.

"Ready?"

"No, I'm running late." She handed him a sandwich and a bottle of water.

"Thanks."

"Are we going to meet at Hank's place?"

"No. He gave me a map of the area he wants us to cover. Chance and Hank are teamed together in a vehicle searching the other side of the ranch. Cade and Travis are on horseback, along with Jarred and Wyatt. You and I are teamed up to check this side of the property."

"Okay, let's go, Captain." She pulled on her all-weather nylon jacket, a scarf and stocking cap for warmth.

He held the door open for her, and she ducked under his arm. He suddenly looked big and intimidating, and deadly serious. She realized this situation could be the same, too. Whoever was shooting at defenseless animals was dangerous.

Outside, they made their way along the path that led up the rise. Even without his cane, Brady didn't seem to have any trouble making the climb up to the parking area. Next to her SUV was the Randell Guest Ranch four-by-four truck. He opened the door and slid into the driver's side. Why not? His right leg was fine.

She got in the passenger side as he bit into his sandwich. That's when his jacket opened and she saw a flash of metal. A gun was tucked into the waistband of his jeans.

"You brought a gun."

He stared the truck. "Yeah, Doc, I did." The flood-light overhead illuminated part of his face. "I hope I don't have to use it." He took another hearty bite and chewed. "But there's no way in hell I'm going out there unarmed." His voice took on a husky quality. "Let's just say it's a precaution."

Lindsey could see the determination in Brady's face and heard it in his voice. He made her feel safe. Besides, they needed to catch whoever was shooting at the mustangs.

She glanced out at the fading daylight. "Where are we supposed to go?"

He handed her the area map from the bench seat between them, then backed the truck out and headed for the highway. "Hank's marked the area he wants us to search."

She looked over the written directions. "Okay, at the highway turn left and go down about a half mile to a service road."

Brady nodded and followed her navigation, trying to concentrate on his job and not think about Lindsey seated so close to him. How was he supposed to do that with her fresh lemon scent filling the small cab? It seemed to wrap around him, trying to distract him, re-minding him how long it had been since he'd been with a woman. A long, long time.

With a groan, he shifted in his seat.

Lindsey turned to him. "You okay? Is your leg hurting you?"

Like hell. "No. I'm just trying to get into a comfortable position. If you can't see the directions, there's a flashlight on the floor."

"I can read just fine. If you'd rather I can drive."

"I said I can handle it," he told her, then finished the last of his sandwich.

"Okay, I'm just trying to help."

"Then read the map," he told her. "And get us to where we need to be."

"Then get ready." She pointed toward the driver's side of the road. "The turn-off should be coming up soon. There it is."

Brady pulled the truck onto the gravel road. After about twenty yards they came to a sign that read, Private Property. No Trespassing. But they soon discovered the gate was already open. "Maybe Hank left it open."

He threw the gearshift in park, reached for the cell phone and punched the buttons.

"This is Hank." Hank's voice came through laced with static. "Have you made it to your location?"

"Not quite. We're at the service road just off the highway. The gate's open. We weren't sure if you'd been here or not."

"Haven't been there in over a week, and none of the ranch hands would leave it open, either."

"Then we'll check it out."

"Call us if you see anything," Hank said. "We'll hightail it over there." There was a pause. "I know you won't walk into anything blindly, but be careful."

"Will do." Brady put the truck in four-wheel drive

and moved cautiously down the road. He felt a rush of excitement. Besides bringing in the mare, this was the first useful thing he'd done in months.

When he came to a fork at the large tree, he slowed, then veered off to the right on the more-traveled road. They went along the uneven dirt path, passing through thick mesquite bushes that were so close they brushed the sides of the truck.

"Do you think this is the right way?" Lindsey asked.

He'd noticed the scratches on the truck when he'd gotten in. "I'd say this is a normal route. Besides, I have no choice but to keep going, even if it's just to turn around." He gave her a quick sideways glance, then returned his attention to the road. He slowed as they came out of the bushes into a grassy clearing. Right away he saw evidence that someone had been there recently.

"Bingo." Brady shut off the engine and got out. Lindsey followed after him. Together, they walked into the remnants of what was once a fire ring, a circle of rocks and some burnt wood.

"Well, someone sure as hell has been here," he said as he walked to the log and found scattered fast-food wrappers and several beer cans along with an empty whiskey bottle. "I'd bet there've been a few parties here."

"I'll call Hank," Lindsey said.

"Good idea." Brady went to the truck and returned with flashlights. He handed her one. "We're losing daylight fast. I'll search the area."

She punched in Hank's number and when he answered, she said, "We found a makeshift campsite about a half mile in. Looks like some kids have been here, and they've been drinking."

"Darn it, I was afraid of that. Is there any sign of anything else?"

"Brady's still looking around."

"Okay, we can be there as soon as we change a flat tire."

Lindsey hung up to see Brady wander off through the high grass. She caught up to him. "Hank will be here as fast he can. Maybe it would be better if you wait for Hank, and don't go out there alone."

He cocked an eyebrow. "Why, Doc, you're worried about me."

"I suspect you can handle yourself okay."

"Thanks for the credit. I've been able to get out of enemy territory, I think I can go look for some simple tracks." He pointed the flashlight down. "And in about ten minutes there'll be no light at all."

"Then I'm coming with you."

She followed after him, letting him lead the way.

He stopped and crouched down, motioning for Lindsey to do the same. "See how the grass is bent?"

She knelt down beside him. His hand pressed against her back, making it hard for her to concentrate on what he was saying.

"I don't think it was done by cattle. Hank doesn't have a herd even close to here. Could be the mustangs, but my guess is they're humans."

"So the shooter was probably here?"

He shrugged as his gaze met hers. "Or it could lead to a place one of the boys took his girl for some privacy." He raised an eyebrow. "A little private make-out place."

She felt the stirring in her stomach and she stood up. "We better keep looking."

Brady stood, too. He concentrated on finding some clues, anything that would prove a shooter was here. They continued to walk through the brush, then came to another clearing and more beer cans.

He aimed his flashlight along the perimeter and caught sight of a shiny object. He knelt down and picked up a brass shell casing, then another. He found a total of three.

"Well, I'll be damned."

Lindsey arrived at his side and looked at his hand. "Shell casings." She looked up at him. "So the shooter was here."

"He was, if these will match the bullet you removed from the mare." He noticed that she was shivering. "Come on, you're cold. Besides, it's too dark to find anything else. We'll wait for Hank." He pocketed the casings and guided her back to the truck.

Once inside, he started the truck and turned on the heater. "Sorry, I didn't notice the drop in temperature."

"It's okay, I'm fine." She smiled, but she was still shivering. "It was worth it. We found this place."

"And we might find who's responsible," he told her. He liked the fact that Lindsey Stafford wasn't afraid to get her hands dirty. He'd watched her yesterday with the mare. Saw firsthand her dedication.

He turned in his seat and leaned back against the door, stretching out his injured leg on the floor. Lindsey was huddled deep in her coat, trying to keep warm. He couldn't stand to watch her shivering.

"Lindsey." He spoke her name and she turned to him. Silently he held out his hands.

"Not a good idea, Brady."

"It's only to keep warm." He reached out and drew her into his arms. Once he opened his coat, she burrowed into his chest seeking warmth. He bit back a groan when her breasts pressed against him. Her hands were splayed against his ribs. He didn't dare take a breath. After a few minutes of heaven, he asked. "Have you gone to sleep on me?"

"No, but I could use some." She turned her head and shifted position slightly. "My beauty sleep was interrupted by someone pounding on my door at dawn."

He smiled, feeling her soft hair against his chin. "I'd say it was for a good reason. Besides, sleeping is highly overrated." He looked down at the woman in his arms. "I can think of more interesting ways to kill the time."

She didn't open her eyes. "Aren't you a little old to be trying to seduce a woman in the woods?"

It was her fault that he'd been thinking like a high school kid. "Hey, there was a time when I could do a lot with some moonlight, a little privacy and a bench seat."

She finally sat up and glared at him. "I bet."

"What can I say? Every teenage boy had one goal in mind."

"I wouldn't know. I didn't date much in school. I was focused on getting into college."

"I'm sure the boys in your school were disappointed."

The faint sound of a song on the radio filled the cab. Even in the darkness, he could feel her eyes on him.

"Hardly, they were more into blondes."

"They were fools." He leaned closer, but Lindsey put up her hand.

"Stop right there."

"Why, darlin', you seemed to like my kisses well enough the other day."

She breathed in a sharp breath. "Well, you didn't give me much of the chance to turn you down."

He studied her cute button nose and stubborn chin. Damn, she was pretty. "You're the one who showed up at my door. To me that said you were interested."

"To you, interested is if a woman breathes."

"I'm more selective than you think. Not just any woman, Doc." He leaned closer and gave in to temptation as he brushed a soft kiss against her lips.

She sucked in a breath, but didn't pull away. "Brady, don't start this. Neither one of us needs this kind of complication."

"You talk too much, Doc. It's cold outside and we need to generate some heat."

"Turn up the heater."

His hand cupped her face and turned her toward him. "How about this instead?" He captured her mouth just as a whimper escaped, but she didn't stop him. It took a few seconds to convince her but slowly her arms went around his neck and she allowed him to slide his tongue inside and taste her.

By the time he broke off the kiss, they both needed air. "Damn, woman, you're dangerous."

She started to pull away and he stopped her.

He leaned forward and nipped at her lower lip, drawing another moan from her. "And I'm a man who lives for danger."

She broke free and sat up. "Well, I don't. So back off fly boy."

He had to admit he wasn't used to this kind of resistance. He held up his hands. "Fine."

Irritated, Brady sat up. That's when he saw the headlights.

Still a little shaky from the kiss, Lindsey managed to get to the other side of the cab and pull herself together.

"Stay here," Brady told her. "It's cold out."

She could only nod when Brady grabbed his hat and climbed out of the truck. She could see he, too, had been affected by the kiss. That wasn't good.

"Hank," Brady called as they got out of the truck.

"What'd you find, son?"

"Over here." They walked to the campsite and shone the flashlights around the area. He handed Hank the casings. "Looks like whoever comes here has been doing it for a while."

Hank didn't look happy. "Well, I'm about to put a stop to it."

"Why not hold off on that for now? Instead, set a trap for them. That way you can let the law handle it. And hopefully stop the problem for good."

Chance stepped in. "What are you thinking of when you say trap?"

"Electronic surveillance." He glanced back at the truck, wanting to get back to Lindsey. "I could come by the ranch and discuss it with you." He glanced back and forth between the men.

"Sounds good," Hank said, but held up his hand. "I just don't want anyone to get hurt. Not us, or those kids. Nothing is worth that." He sighed. "So stop by tomorrow and we'll see if we can agree on a way to handle this."

Brady nodded. "Sounds good."

"Now, go and take Lindsey home. And thanks for the help."

They said their goodbyes, and Hank waved to Lindsey in the truck, then drove off with Chance.

Brady climbed into the warm cab, shifted into gear and followed the other truck out. "Looks like you got your wish, Lindsey. I can take you home and get you in bed."

"My, Captain, aren't you taking a lot for granted?"

He grinned and winked at her. Her heart tripped in her chest and she couldn't find any more words to say.

She was in big trouble.

Lindsey didn't talk on the drive back to the cabin. It had been a mistake going with Brady tonight, and letting him kiss her again was even more stupid. It was time to end any involvement with the man. Not give him encouragement, because in the end he'd walk away when he learned her connection to Jack Randell. The real reason she'd come here.

When they pulled into the parking area, Lindsey tried to get out of the truck before Brady could follow her. She wanted no repeat of what happened earlier. No more kissing Brady Randell was her recited mantra.

But the stubborn captain refused to take no for an answer and walked her to the well-lit porch. She unlocked the door but didn't go inside. Instead she turned around to face Brady. "Okay, I'm safely home. You can go now."

He leaned an arm against the doorjamb. "Look, Doc, I know you're ticked off at me right now, but if the truth be told, you were into that kiss just as much as I was."

"I'm not talking about this to you. So you need to go." She didn't want to admit how much she was drawn to him. "All I want is some sleep. My day starts early tomorrow."

Brady shifted his stance. He didn't have to get up at all, if he didn't want to. Even though his leg was throbbing like crazy, he didn't want to go back to the cottage and sit there alone watching some meaningless late-night television.

He raised a hand to argue when her cell phone went off. She pulled it from her coat pocket. "Dr. Stafford," she answered.

Brady watched her forehead wrinkle in a frown.

"I should be there in about twenty minutes," she said as she went inside and picked up a pen off the counter. "Give me the directions," she said, then began to jot down the instructions. "Yes, I know the road. Okay." She nodded. "I'm on my way." She flipped the phone closed.

"What's wrong?"

"The Carson's mare is having trouble birthing her foal. I've got to get out there." She hurried into the kitchen area, grabbed a bottle of water from the refrigerator and headed for the door.

"Need some help?" he called to her when he caught up with her on the driver's side of her SUV. "It's been a while, but I helped my dad a few times with calves."

She stopped. "It's a messy job and could take hours."

He smiled. "I'm your man, Doc."

That was what she was afraid of.

CHAPTER FIVE

THIS was getting to be a habit.

Brady was behind the wheel of her SUV, and Lindsey sat in the passenger seat, giving directions to the ranch. It took nearly twenty minutes to get to the Carson's place. A boy about ten stood by the road and flagged them down, then pointed toward the barn. That was where they found the boy's mother, Bonnie Carson, with her quarter horse.

In the oversize stall, the young mare was already down, her head cradled in her owner's lap, and visibly in distress. Lindsey knelt on the fresh straw floor.

"Mrs. Carson, I'm Dr. Stafford. This is Brady Randell."

"I can't tell you how glad I am to see you, Doctor, Mr. Randell."

Lindsey could hear the fatigue and fear in the woman's voice. "This here is Under the Mistletoe. We call her Missy."

Lindsey studied the laboring mare. "How long has Missy been down?"

"She's been up and down for the last few hours, but

this time it's been about ten to fifteen minutes. My husband would have been here, but he's stranded at the Denver Airport." There was a tremor in her voice. "Of course Missy chose now to go into labor." She nodded to her son. "Buddy has helped his dad, so I thought we could handle it. Then when Missy didn't seem to be getting anywhere, I called you."

Lindsey felt a strong contraction, and the horse's head came up and she let out a whinny. She soothed the animal until she calmed again. "It's okay, girl. We'll figure out what's taking so long." She looked at Bonnie. "I'll know more after I examine her."

Lindsey stood and went to her large case, not wanting to say out loud her suspicions that the foal might be breech.

Brady stood next to her. "What can I do?"

His voice was reassuring, and she was suddenly glad he was here with her. "You can bring me those clean towels and keep them handy." Stripping off her jacket, she nodded to the stack on a trunk outside the stall. She opened her medical bag and hung her stethoscope around her neck, then worked a waterless disinfectant over her hands and arms, took out a pair of latex gloves and slipped them on.

"I'll need you to go help Mrs. Carson, make sure that Missy stays down while I examine her."

"Done." Brady grabbed the towels and stacked them close by, then took his position to help the owner.

Lindsey knelt down and checked the horse's heart rate. Definitely fast. All the while she continued to talk softly as she slipped her hand inside the womb. She grimaced when she discovered the answer to the mare's long labor.

She sat back on her heels. "There's good news and bad," she said to Bonnie Carson. "The foal isn't a standard breech, but the legs are back. I need to bring them forward."

She looked at Brady. "Hold her still again." Their gaze met and he nodded, feeling a knot tighten his chest. He'd do his damnedest for her.

After another contraction, Lindsey reached back inside as far as her arm would allow and managed to get hold of one of the foal's legs. She pulled it forward. "Got one."

She looked at Brady and he sent her an encouraging wink. A little shiver rippled through her.

"Come on, Doc, one more to go," he whispered. "You can do it."

She had to glance away. That was when she spotted the preteen boy and a little girl peering between the stall railings. She didn't have to wonder what this horse meant to them.

Everyone went silent as if their concentration could help her search for the missing limb. It seemed to take forever, then she finally located it. "There you are." She maneuvered the leg in position as tears filled her eyes.

Entranced, Brady watched the intense focus on her face as she worked to help the mare. He soon discovered she was stronger than he could imagine. Beads of sweat popped on her forehead as she did her job. He could see her determination. With the next contraction, her efforts paid off when the mucus-covered hooves appeared.

"Come on, Missy." Tears filled Bonnie's eyes as she coaxed the horse to continue the birthing. With

Lindsey's assistance the foal slid out into the world. The kids cheered as Lindsey wiped the reddish-colored filly with a towel and nudged her to stand.

"Good job, Doc," Brady said. He was surprised to see Lindsey's blush, then her attention went back to her other patient.

"Missy did all the work." She patted the still-down mare. "Take a rest, girl, you deserve it."

Ten minutes later a mother's instinct took over and the horse stood to check out her baby.

"Thank you so much, Doctor," Bonnie said. "I was so afraid we were going to lose them both."

"I'm glad you called me." She turned to the kids. "Have you two come up with a name yet?"

They shrugged shyly, then the boy said, "Maybe we can call her Doc Lindsey."

Two hours later they finally got back in the truck, Lindsey didn't even bother fighting Brady for the keys. She closed her eyes and leaned back against the headrest, feeling exhausted and exhilarated at the same time.

"Was this your first?" Brady asked. "Your first breech, I mean."

"Did it show?"

"No. You did an incredible job."

"Until tonight, I've only assisted in breech deliveries. Not that I would have told Bonnie Carson that."

"Well, mama and baby are doing fine. That's all that counts," Brady said.

His compliment meant a lot to her. "Thanks. And thank you for your help, too."

"Why? You did all the work."

"Keeping a large horse calm is a big help, but especially with a first-time mother, it isn't easy."

He reached across the seat, took her hand and squeezed it. "Just glad I was there for you."

She found she liked his reassuring touch. She needed it right now; she needed him. How easy it would be to let go. Even though he had danger written all over him, she would eagerly welcome his attention, his strength…his heart-stopping kisses. She sighed deeply.

Who was she kidding? Brady Randell was already buried deep into her thoughts. A man any woman would desire, and she was no exception.

Even if she wasn't truly related to Jack Randell, it still wouldn't be safe to get involved with a man who would leave her when his time here was up.

He'd go back to his first love, flying.

Brady pulled into the parking lot. "Home, safe and sound." He looked at her from across the car, and she quickly climbed out to avoid temptation.

He came around the car and gave her the keys, then slipped his hands in the front pockets of his jeans. "It's been quite a night, Doc. Thanks for letting me tag along."

"I need to thank you again, Brady. You were a big help." Lindsey needed to get away from the man, before she made a big mistake. "You really don't have to walk me down to my door. I know your leg has to be hurting."

"It's not a problem."

Shaking her head, she started to back away, praying he wouldn't pursue her. "You can watch from here to see that I get inside safely."

He looked disappointed but nodded. "Well, Doc, it's been an interesting evening to say the least." He took a step closer, but Lindsey wasn't about to let him kiss her. Oh, no, she'd be a goner for sure.

"Good night." She turned and hurried down the slope, then tossed him a wave as she opened the cabin door. She sighed with relief when he saluted back and headed for Hank's truck.

Once inside, she shut the door with a final click. She was alone. Brady was gone. Maybe for good. Suddenly she felt the absolute loneliness rush over her.

In the past ten years, she'd concentrated on school and her career. There hadn't been time in her life for a man. Not that she missed it. She hadn't found anyone yet who made her heart race, made her breath catch. Until now.

Until Brady Randell.

He wasn't the answer, she told herself. He didn't want commitment, or a future with a woman. He was the love-'em-and-leave-'em type. He got his thrills from piloting a F-16 thousands of feet over the earth. He was just killing time, hanging around and flirting with her.

"So get any silly thoughts out of your head," she told herself as she headed to the bedroom, stripping off her dirty sweater. Removing her boots, she kicked free from her jeans and tossed them in the corner, deciding to deal with them in the morning. She looked longingly at the huge canopy bed with the thick satin comforter that was definitely made for two, as was the large sunken tub in the bathroom. She pushed aside any thoughts of sharing these amenities with a man.

Right now she needed sleep. Grabbing a pair of pajamas from the drawer, she slipped on the cotton bottoms and was tying the drawstring when she heard the knock on the door.

She glanced at the clock. It was after midnight. Far too late for anyone to come by. She slipped on her T-shirt and robe, then hurried to the door.

"Who is it?"

"Brady."

She closed her eyes. "Look, Brady, I'm tired."

"Believe me, I'd like to be home and in a warm bed, too. But the truck won't start."

She opened the door, and cool air hit her. Brady Randell was huddled in his coat. She could see his breath. "What's wrong with it?"

"As far as I can tell it's a dead battery. I think I left the dome light on."

Lindsey realized she'd been the one who turned it on in the first place. She stepped aside to let him in. "Come inside where it's warm."

"Look, I hate to bother you, but I can't call Hank this late. Could you loan me your car to get home, and I'll bring it back in the morning?"

"Could you get it back by six?" she asked. "I have an appointment at seven."

He groaned, then glanced at the sofa in front of the fireplace. "Then I'll guess I'll just bunk down here for the night, okay?"

She saw the fatigue and pain etching his face and didn't have the heart—or the energy—to turn him away. "I'll get you some blankets."

He was in trouble.

Brady gripped the throttle hard, but he still couldn't control the vibration. In his head, he ran through the aircraft's checklist, reminding himself over and over that he was an experienced pilot. He'd been able to bring in crippled planes before, but his instincts told him this was different. For one, he wasn't over friendly territory.

Another warning light screamed. The jet was losing altitude. Fast. His heart pounded hard in his chest, he sucked in oxygen, fought the panic.

He was going down.

The only safety net he had was his communication with ground control. He made his Mayday call.

He was left with no choice but to eject. There wasn't any time left to think about it. He reached for the yellow-and-black-striped handle, said a quick prayer and yanked hard. He gasped at the powerful force that shot him upward. He cried out, and everything went black.

"Brady! Brady! Wake up!"

He gasped for air and jerked up. Oh, God. He blinked away sleep and saw Lindsey's face. He groaned.

"Are you okay?" she asked.

He worked to slow his breathing and lied with a nod. "Sorry. I didn't mean to wake you." He tried to turn away. "Please, go back to bed."

She touched his arm, causing his gaze to meet hers. "Were you dreaming about the crash?"

"It's not a big deal." He lifted his shoulders. "It happens sometimes."

Brady watched her stand up. A part of him hoped she would leave him alone. Another part ached to pull her down and hold her.

She went into the dimly lit kitchen and returned with a bottle of water. She handed it to him, then sat down on the floor in front of the sofa.

He took a hearty drink, then blew out a breath. After

finishing off the water, he dropped his head back on the pillow. "Please, Lindsey, go back to bed."

"I want to make sure you're okay."

"I'm fine." He closed his eyes.

"If you tell me about it, I might be able to help."

He released another sigh. "The way I'm feeling right now, Doc, I want a hellava lot more than just your sympathy. So if you know what's good for you, you better leave. Now."

Lindsey had been warned, so why didn't she go? She examined his solid and well-developed chest. He had the kind of six-pack abs most men only dream about.

Not only was he every woman's fantasy, he looked more than capable of taking care of himself. But there was something in those dark, brooding eyes that wouldn't let her leave him. His body might be healing quickly from his accident, but what about his soul?

"Lindsey, I said go…."

"Since when do you give the orders?" she tried to joke. "Besides, I'm awake now. So I guess you're stuck with me. You told me the other day you loved early mornings. So do I. To see the sun come up when every-thing is so fresh and new." She reached out a hand and touched his bare arm, not surprised to feel the sheen of sweat on his warm skin, the subtle tremble. He wasn't totally naked. He still had on his jeans.

Not much of a barrier, she warned herself, and she let her hand drop away. "There are times when we need to know that we're not alone, Brady."

"And sometimes we need to be by ourselves to think things through."

"And sometimes we *over*think things," she countered.

"Easy for you to say. I have to go through a Medical Review Board and let them decide if I'm fit to fly again. And nightmares don't help my cause."

She was surprised at his admission. "Brady, it's okay to be afraid sometimes." She'd been there so many times herself. "I used to have nightmares. I was scared all the time, but nighttime was the worst of all. I was so afraid to close my eyes."

Brady rolled on his side and propped his head in his hand. "Afraid monsters would get you?"

"Yeah. But this monster was very real. My father." She shivered, hating that she still held on to the memories. "He liked to drink. And when he drank, he got mean...and nasty."

This time Brady reached for her hand and he gently squeezed her fingers.

"He used to take it out on my mother mostly."

Brady cursed. "Tell me he didn't come after you."

She shrugged. "A few times he tried. My mom stopped him, then she paid a big price for it." She felt the tears in her voice.

He growled. "Man, that's rough, Doc."

She shook her head. "No, I didn't tell you so you'd feel sorry for me. Just to let you know that we all have nightmares, Brady. And it's always worse when we're alone." She wasn't sure if she was speaking for him or herself.

"I'm glad you're here." He tugged on her hand, bringing her closer as he leaned toward her. "What I'm going to do right now has nothing to do with my nightmare. I'm going to kiss you, Doc. So if you want me to stop, let me know right now."

She didn't say a word.

His mouth descended on hers before Lindsey could resist. Not that she wanted to, because kissing Brady Randell was like nothing she'd ever experienced before. The feelings he created in her were unbelievable.

He groaned and coaxed her up to lie down beside him on the sofa. He pulled her closer and deepened the kiss, tasting her thoroughly. She knew this wasn't wise, but she wanted this man so much, she refused to listen to common sense.

Her body quaked as he pulled her under him. She whimpered, feeling the wonderful weight of him. She sensed a new tension in his body as his hands went to work pleasuring her. He caressed her skin beneath her T-shirt, causing her to arch up, offering him her breasts. When he finally touched her, she gasped, bracing herself for the sensation he caused as he lifted her shirt and his lips drew a nipple into his eager mouth.

She cried out.

"Lindsey… I can't seem to keep away from you." His mouth returned to hers, the kisses became more and more intense.

Lindsey's hand moved over Brady's back, then bravely she slipped her fingers inside his jeans, finding his taut bottom.

With a groan, he raised his head and tugged her against his chest, skin to skin. "I've got to feel you against me, Doc." His gaze met hers reflecting his heated desire. "I want you."

Her heart drummed in her chest. She wanted him, too. "Brady…"

"We've been dancing around these feelings since we met. You want this, too, Doc."

She opened her mouth to speak, but her cell phone began to ring. "I've got to answer that."

With a groan he raised his arm, letting her get up.

Lindsey scrambled off the sofa, pulling her clothes back together as she grabbed the phone from the table. "Hello."

"Well good morning, Lin." At the sound of Jack's voice, Lindsey fought her panic but lost. She looked at the bare-chested Brady lying on the sofa and mouthed, "I need to take this call."

She nearly changed her mind on seeing the desire in his eyes, but common sense took over. She turned away and walked into the bedroom and closed the door.

"Jack, is something wrong?" A dozen things raced through her head, none good.

"No, but we're wondering about you. Your mother and I haven't heard from you."

"That's because you're on the trip of a lifetime. Who wants their kid calling all the time to check up on them?"

There was a long pause. "C'mon, Lin, we love hearing from you. And since you weren't answering at your apartment, we were kind of concerned."

She blew out a breath as she paced the bedroom. "I went to visit Kelly Grant," she said, which wasn't exactly a lie. She had gone to stay with her college friend nearly a month ago. "And I've been checking out some job prospects."

"That's good. Find anything interesting?"

"I'm not sure." She tried to change the subject. "How was your trip?"

"It was great. We got back yesterday. And if you

come home this weekend we'll fill you in on everything and bore you with pictures."

Lindsey could hear the fatigue in her stepfather's voice. Had he told Mom the truth yet?

"We'd really love to see you."

"I can't this weekend, Jack. I've got a few interviews coming up. But I'll be home for Thanksgiving."

There was a hesitation, then Jack said, "I told your mother…everything. We talked most of the night and she finally fell asleep."

Tears filled her eyes. "Oh, Jack. How did she take it?"

"As well as can be expected. I know it would do her good to see you."

"And she'll get to. I promise I'll be there for her." She held her emotions in check. "You know I'll do anything I can to help you both."

"I know, Lin." There was another pause. "But there might not be any options this time. And you and your mother have to accept that."

"There are still some alternatives out there, Jack."

"Not as far as I'm concerned."

"How do you know if you don't try?"

"Please, Lin, don't push this. This is the way it has to be."

She knew the man was stubborn, but so was she. "Okay, I'll let it go for now. Tell Mom I love her and I'll call her later. I love you, Jack." She wiped the tears from her face.

"Love you, too, Lin."

She hung up the phone. Dear Lord, how was she going to convince him to come here? She turned and found Brady standing in the doorway.

She gasped. "I'm sorry the call took so long."

"Not a problem. Are you okay?" He came to her, and brushed a tear off her face. "I take it that wasn't a business call."

She shook her head. "It was my stepfather. My parents just got back from a cruise."

Lindsey was rambling, but if she stopped she'd end up back in his arms. Bury herself in his strength, but it would be fleeting. There couldn't be a repeat of that. Brady would be gone soon.

Lindsey stepped back from the temptation. "I should get ready for work."

Brady glanced at the clock. "You still have two hours. Are you sure you're just not afraid of what nearly happened between us."

She stiffened. "I need to get you home."

"I can call Hank or Luke." His eyebrows drew together. "Is everything okay with your family?"

Lindsey swallowed. "Yes. I'm going home for Thanksgiving."

She didn't want Brady Randell to be nice to her. She didn't want to like the man who just moments ago had been doing a good job of seducing her. The most important thing she needed to remember was that her stepfather, Jack, was also Brady's uncle.

And when she finally came clean about her true reason for coming here, the entire Randell family might just band together and run her out of town. Brady was a Randell. His loyalty would lie with his family.

She nodded. "If you don't mind, I need to take a shower."

He studied her for a long moment, then turned and walked away.

Lindsey had to fight hard to keep from calling him back. Then she reminded herself that he was only around temporarily, just like she was. In the end, they'd both go back to their separate lives. She thought about the scene on the sofa. Of the hunger of Brady's kisses, the incredible touch of his hands on her body. She drew a breath and closed her eyes, vowing not to let things go any further.

She knew she couldn't keep that promise.

Thirty minutes later the sun was up, a pot of strong coffee was on. Brady probably should have called Hank and let him know about the truck, but he decided he wasn't ready to leave Lindsey Stafford. She presented herself as a tough, independent veterinarian, but he knew better. After she'd told him about her father's abuse, he had a feeling that her stepdad was the man who'd been there for her.

Damn. He shouldn't get involved in any one else's problems. Brady took another sip of coffee. He had enough to concentrate on with his career and adapting to a place in his new family. That was about all he could handle right now.

When the door to the bedroom opened, he turned to see Lindsey. She had on fresh jeans and a white blouse under a navy sweater. Her auburn hair was shiny and curled against her shoulders.

She glanced around the living room, then turned toward the kitchen. He smiled and held up a mug of coffee.

"You looking for this?"

She blinked in surprise. "I wouldn't mind a cup." She came toward him and took her mug. "I can't function without caffeine."

Brady agreed. "I need that extra kick in the morning, too. If you had more time I would have treated you to my famous cinnamon pancakes." He grinned. "Maybe next time."

She stopped her mug's journey to her mouth. "Sorry, Captain, there isn't going to be a next time."

He faced her. "Oh, Doc, that's the one thing I am sure about. Things aren't settled between us. So there's definitely going to be a next time."

CHAPTER SIX

ABOUT an hour later, Lindsey pulled up at the foreman's cottage to drop off Brady. What she didn't expect to find was his brother, Luke, Tess and another woman Lindsey didn't recognize standing on the porch.

"Please, tell me you called your brother to let him know what happened with Hank's truck."

"It was too late last night, and I guess I forgot about it this morning."

"You better think about answering some questions, because to them it's going to look like we spent the night together."

He looked at her and grinned. "We did. Technically."

"This isn't a game, Brady." She shifted the SUV into park not far from the porch. "I'm trying to build a reputation here."

His smile died. "So let's not tarnish it by letting people think you spent the night with a washed-up jet jockey." He pushed open the door.

Lindsey grabbed his arm. "Brady, you know that's not what I meant. I like to keep my private life private."

"Don't worry, Doc. I'll stay clear of you from now

on." He slammed the door and started toward the porch.

With a frustrated sigh, Lindsey hit the steering wheel. She hadn't meant to hurt his feelings, but that's exactly what she'd done. At the very least she'd stepped on his ego. She climbed out of the car and leaned against the hood. "Oh, Brady," she called out. "Thank you for last night."

He stopped, but didn't turn around. She didn't miss the tension in his broad shoulders.

She poured it on. "I had a great time. Call me anytime." With a wave to Luke and Tess on the porch, she got back into the car and drove off, calling herself crazy. Why should she care what Brady Randell thought?

Darn it, she did.

Brady walked up the pathway to the porch, surprised to feel a heat climbing up his neck. Lindsey had just let people think there was something going on between them. He suddenly smiled. So he was getting to her.

"Good morning, Luke, Tess. Hi, Brenna." He arched an eyebrow. "Am I late for my session?"

The cute therapist smiled. "Not for an hour or so. I came by to visit with Tess."

"Good, I'd like a chance to shower and change."

"I'll be back, though." She nodded to his injured leg. "How's the leg doing since our last workout?"

"Okay."

"All right, see you later." She and Tess headed up to the main house.

Luke stayed back. "I don't want to track your every move, but it would nice if you answered your cell phone."

Brady pulled it out and saw that the battery was

dead. "I guess I didn't think about it. We were too busy looking for the guys who shot the mustang. When I took Lindsey home, she had an emergency call and I went along to help deliver a foal. By the time we got back, the battery in Hank's truck had died. So I spent the night at the cabin."

His brother nodded. "So you're seeing Lindsey?"

"I spent yesterday with her, but that isn't exactly 'seeing.' Why? You have a problem with that?"

Luke shrugged. "It's not my business what you do. I was just trying to have a conversation with my brother. And I want to help see that you heal and get back to what you want to do, fly. Isn't that what you want, too?"

For the first time Brady hesitated. "That doesn't mean I can't enjoy a beautiful woman's company while I'm here."

"I just don't want to see anyone get hurt."

Brady headed for the door as his brother stepped off the porch. "Look, Lindsey was joking around when she said what she said. I spent the night on her sofa." Not that it was where he'd wanted to be. He recalled how good it had felt when she'd come to check on him. How good she felt to hold. "You don't have to worry about her."

His brother stared at him. "Who says Lindsey is the one I'm worried about?"

"Do five more...but take it slower, then hold it," Brenna said. "That's it."

Brady fought a groan. He lay on the workout table in one of the cottage bedrooms, after taking off his removable booted cast from his leg, he'd strapped weights to his ankle as he did leg lifts.

Luke had made sure that there was enough equipment to help his younger brother stay in shape. And Brady had taken full advantage by working out the frustration of being confined to the house.

Although Brenna Gentry looked small and unassuming, she was strong as the dickens, working him through the isometric exercises and some light weight lifting. He wanted more. He wanted to get back to normal. And fast.

"Slow down," she told him, and grabbed hold of his leg as he pumped the weight. "You overdo and you could lose ground." She rolled those pretty brown eyes. "What am I saying? I normally have to prod my patients to work harder. But you I can't hold back."

"I want to get this over and be normal again."

"You'll get there, Brady," she told him. "You've made great progress."

"Not fast enough." He sat up and took the towel she offered. "It's been months since my accident."

"It's been three months. And you're coming along as scheduled."

"It's just not *my* schedule," he said.

"Then talk to your doctor at the next visit. Maybe he can give you a better idea."

"I plan to." He studied the pretty woman. "Thanks for all your help, Brenna. I couldn't have gotten this far without you."

"Don't you know I'm a sucker for Randell men?"

Brady hadn't had much of a chance to get to know his cousins. He'd heard a little about Dylan Gentry having been a bull rider. His career had ended after a bad spill off one mean bull. "You better not let your husband hear you say that. I don't need him coming after me."

She smiled. "Oh, I wouldn't worry so much. He's long past those wild days. He's practically a stay-at-home dad now."

His cousins and his brother all seemed content with their lives, happily married and with children. Brady had never stayed in one place long enough to want that. Growing up, family had been him and his mother. His dad was away too much.

"Well, I hope he realizes what he's got."

Her smile grew mischievous. "Oh, he knows, all right. But hey, feel free to tell him yourself if you come to Thanksgiving."

He frowned. "I don't do holidays." He thought about Lindsey being gone.

"You will now, Captain. But relax, it's not the entire family. This is the off year. Most wives around are going to the in-laws. Since my family will be gone, Tess invited us here along with a few others. So you aren't meeting everyone, yet. That will come a little later." She leaned back against the treadmill. "So Thanksgiving will only be about twenty or so."

"How many kids?"

Well, there's Livy. You know she's planning on marrying you."

"Very funny."

Brenna shook her head. "You're just like all the rest of your cousins, Brady Randell. No matter what age, the women flock to you."

The only woman Brady wanted was determined to hold him at an arm's length. "I prefer my ladies over the age of consent. Anyway, I'm married to the air force. And I like my women willing, but not long-term."

"I've heard that before," Brenna said. "Even a world-champion bull rider, Dylan 'Dare Devil' Gentry had succumbed to love of the right woman." With a knowing smile, she headed toward the door and called out, "See you later."

Whoa, just because his cousins and brother found marriage agreeable didn't mean the institution was for him. He'd never given much thought about a wife and kids. It had always been the military, his career. He'd known men who'd done it, handled a family and flying. His dad hadn't been one of them.

Georgia Randell had been on her own more often than with her husband during their marriage. Maybe that had been the reason Brady hadn't sought out a long-term relationship. Or was it the fact that he'd just never met a woman who made him want to change his priorities?

Surprisingly, his thoughts turned to Lindsey.

A week later Lindsey had returned from Thanksgiving with her parents. It had been the first time in memory she'd hadn't wanted to be home for a holiday. It was hard to see her mother's sadness. It was also hard to keep her secret from them. She'd managed to get through it and was now more determined than ever to talk with Jack's boys.

Her first call was at the Rocking R to check on Tess's stallion. In truth she hoped she'd run into Brady. She hadn't been able to get him out of her thoughts since she'd dropped him off after their night together. She kept playing it over in her head, the hungry kisses, the way he'd touched her. Brady had distracted her from thinking about everything else.

Lindsey climbed out of her SUV and headed toward the barn, forcing herself not to look toward the cottage. On her trek through the corral, she tried to stay focused on important things like the reason she'd come to San Angelo. The reason she still needed to talk about with the Randells. And she was running out of time. What was more important, Jack was running out of time.

Inside the barn she went toward Whiskey's stall and set down her case. The animal greeted her eagerly.

"Hi, boy," she crooned, thinking about her mother and what she'd been going through.

Gail Randell was strong and independent, and she loved Jack fiercely. For the past eighteen years, they'd been each other's salvation. After her mother's abusive relationship with her first husband finally ended, she'd been left with next to nothing and a ten-year-old daughter to raise.

One day Jack had shown up at the ranch. He'd just been released from prison and needed a job. With little money, her mom hired him. Over time, Jack told them about his past, his sons and all the mistakes he'd made in his lifetime.

It took years, but together they built a thriving horse-breeding business and—in the meantime—fell in love. And now Jack could possibly die. Tears threatened, and Lindsey quickly blinked them away. She wasn't ready to lose him. Not for a long, long time.

"Lindsey."

She swung around to see Brady walking toward her,

his booted cast strapped around his lower leg. He still looked good dressed in jeans and his familiar flight jacket. That was when she realized she'd been attracted to him from the first time she laid eyes on the handsome pilot. She'd missed him.

"Oh, Brady. Hi."

He didn't smile back. "Is something wrong?"

She shook her head. "I needed to check Whiskey."

He frowned. "That's right, you've been gone."

"Just over Thanksgiving." She smiled. "My mom made a big fuss with a turkey, dressing and tons of pies. How about you?"

He shrugged. "I spent it with Luke and Tess and a few assorted cousins."

Had he missed her not being around? Probably not.

She glanced away from his stare. "It's nice to have family."

"Haven't decided that yet. I'm not into big crowds."

She knew he was still getting used to the Randells. If she'd learned anything since being here, it was that the Randells could be a little overwhelming. Not that she wouldn't love to be a part of their clan.

"Well, speaking for myself," she began, "I'd never turn down all that turkey and dressing. And, oh, the pies." She sighed. "Pumpkin's my favorite, but I wouldn't say no to pecan or warm apple pie with tons of whipped cream."

Brady had trouble not reacting to Lindsey's enthusiasm, and he wasn't talking about the food. Well, maybe the whipped cream. He grabbed her by the hand and led her the short distance to the tack room.

"Brady, this isn't a good idea," she began as he shut the door behind them.

He looked into her gorgeous eyes, and a thrill shot through him as he drew her into his arms. "Hell, I know that. But I've wanted to do this since that night at your cabin. It's been too damn long." He bent his head and captured her mouth.

Lindsey made him forget everything, but she also made him feel things. Things he didn't have any business feeling, things that went beyond need, desire, gratification. Nothing had prepared him for Lindsey Stafford.

Brady broke off the kiss, willing himself to slow his breathing. "Just a little something to make sure you haven't forgotten about me." He stared into her incredible green eyes and nearly lost it again.

He didn't wait for a response, his mouth closed over hers again. Her soft moan stirred him as his hands went inside her jacket and began to move over her luscious curves. He had about enough brain power left to realize where this was leading. He pulled back and took a breath, seeing her mouth swollen from his kisscs. His gaze moved to her blouse, the rise and fall of her breasts.

"Damn!" He backed away. He didn't need someone like Lindsey in his life, but that didn't stop him wanting her.

She blushed. "We seem to get in these situations…" she began.

"Situations!" he groaned. "Situation? Hell, woman, we practically go up in flames whenever we're together."

Lindsey glanced away. "Then it's better if we stay away from each other."

Before Brady could agree wholeheartedly, he heard his name called out. What now? He shot her one last look, then went out the door to find his sister-in-law coming down the aisle.

"Brady. I've been looking for you."

"What's up?"

"I wanted to remind you about the family dinner at Hank's place tonight."

Brady bit back a curse. "Look, Tess, I don't think I can handle—"

She rested her hand on her hips. "Brady, they're having this dinner for you. Come on, we weren't able to all get together at Thanksgiving and this is the best time. We're just family." Her gaze wandered toward the tack room door to see Lindsey walk out. "Oh…Lindsey. Hi. Sorry I wasn't here to meet you."

"That's okay. I was just starting to examine Whiskey."

Tess nodded, but she wasn't fooled over the story. "I'm glad you're here because I wanted to extend an invitation to you for tonight, too."

Lindsey shook her head. "No, no, I'm not intruding on family. But you need to go, Brady."

Brady liked Tess's idea. "Not without you."

Tess smiled. "Well, you two work it out. Just be at Hank's place about six." She disappeared down the aisle.

Once they were alone, Brady turned toward Lindsey. "Look, I'm not into family things. So if you go, some of the focus will be off me."

"And on me," she said. "And there's another problem, Brady, everyone will think we're a couple."

"Of course. It's only natural you'd be attracted to a devastatingly handsome fighter pilot."

She fought a smile. "Oh, really?"

He grinned. "They're going to speculate, anyway. Why not let them?"

He saw the doubt in those eyes. "Brady, you really think that settles it?"

"Oh, Doc, as far as I'm concerned, this is far from being settled."

Brady was a coward. He'd faced danger at 10,000 feet, but meeting the entire Randell clan terrified him. He'd met all the cousins at one time or the other, but never all together.

"Relax, Brady. This isn't a firing squad," Lindsey said, sitting in the passenger seat in his brother's BMW.

"That might be easier than the series of questions I'm going to get tonight."

That had been one of the reasons he'd wanted to bring Lindsey, hoping it would direct attention off him.

"Big tough guy like you can handle it," she said. "Besides, you're good-looking and charming, so the women will love you. You're a fighter pilot, so the men will be envious, and the kids will go crazy to hear your stories."

He couldn't help but grin. "You think I'm good-looking?"

She glared at him. "Like that's something you don't know. But maybe I did go a bit overboard when I used the word *charming*."

He drove under the Circle B Ranch archway. "Sorry, it's too late to take it back."

"The one thing you don't lack is ego," she told him.

He'd known a lot of women, but none like Lindsey.

He knew that might not be a good thing. He parked next to the trucks that lined the new barnlike structure. He shut off the engine and turned to her.

"Hey, I know who I am." He thumbed his chest. "A damn good fighter pilot. Would you want anyone but the best defending your country?"

Her green eyes locked with his. "No. I only want the best."

He gave her his best cocky grin. "You got him, Doc." Brady climbed out of the car to help her. His gaze moved over her. She wore a pair of black slacks and a rust-colored sweater under a black leather jacket. Her hair was pulled up away from her face showing off hoop earrings.

"You look nice tonight."

"Thank you. I should have brought something."

"We brought wine." He pulled the bag out of the backseat. "I'm sure the ladies will like that."

Lindsey took a deep breath and released it. She shouldn't have come. Although technically she was a stepsister and stepcousin. As far as the Randells knew she was the new veterinarian. And there was a possibility that if the Randells discovered her deception, she wouldn't be invited back.

Hank walked toward them, smiling. "Hello, Lindsey."

"Hello, Hank," she said.

He turned to Brady. "And the guest of honor."

"If you keep saying that, I'm going to leave. There was no need for this get-together."

The older man laughed. "You don't know women very well. Come on, you two, let's go and see everyone."

They entered the large structure that had been built

a few years back and used as the guest ranch's meeting hall with a cafeteria-style kitchen. In one section, there were linen-covered tables decorated for the party.

The noise level was nearly deafening as several kids ran around chasing each other, having a good time. Lindsey had already met several of the brothers, but not all the wives.

"Hey, cuz, it's nice you made it." Chance pulled a pretty blonde against his side. "You haven't had the pleasure of meeting my wife, Joy. Joy, this is Brady and Dr. Lindsey Stafford."

"Hello, Joy," Brady said.

"Brady, Lindsey, it's nice to finally meet you both." She pointed to a name tag across her upper chest and then handed them theirs already filled in. "This should simplify things a little."

"I appreciate that," Lindsey said as she saw Brenna Gentry standing with Tess across the room. She smiled and sent a friendly wave toward them.

Lindsey took a breath and released it as she stole a glance at Jack's other sons. She'd gotten a big shock the other day when she learned about Jarred Trager and Wyatt and Dylan Gentry. Lindsey believed with all her heart that Jack deserved to know about them.

Chance's voice interrupted her thoughts. "We'll take a pass on giving all the children's names—"

"That's because you can't name them all," his brother Cade said as he handed Brady a beer.

Chance glared. "No, I just think their parents should handle it. This family can be a little much all at once."

"You think?" he murmured, and took a drink from his longneck bottle.

Hank and Ella stepped into the circle. "Welcome to the family, Brady."

Hank didn't forget her, either. "Welcome, too, Lindsey. Glad you could make it."

"Thank you for inviting me to share in your family dinner."

The older man frowned. "You'll always be welcome here. We have a saying, 'You don't have to be blood to be in this family.'" He nodded. "And our hope is that you'll want to be a permanent part of our community, too. We want you to stay on here."

She wanted that, too, but she couldn't, not until things were settled for her. "Honestly, I have been thinking about it." She couldn't make a decision yet. "Thank you so much for the offer." She saw Tess setting food on the table. "I think I'll go help the women." She walked off before anyone could stop her.

Brady's gaze followed Lindsey. He wondered why she was so evasive about Hank's offer.

Suddenly he saw the group of kids gathering. He had his own problems to worry about.

"Uncle Brady," Livy called as she ran to him.

He couldn't help but smile as the cute five-year-old came up to him along with another group of little girls. "Hi, Uncle Brady."

"Hello, princess." He bent over to her level.

"These are my cousins, Sarah Ann, Cassie and Kristin."

"Hello, ladies. My, aren't you all looking pretty."

His words drew girlish giggles.

Interest grew as more of the younger generation wandered over. The boys. "Who do we have here?"

Livy took over the introductions again. "This is Evan

and he's nine years old." She pointed to a tall, lanky boy. "Jeff is fourteen." Another tall teenager. "Brandon is the oldest, and he's nineteen. His brother is James Henry and he's seven. All the rest are with their mommies."

"It's nice to meet you all." Brady held out his hand and shook the boys' hands.

It was Jeff who spoke first. "Are you really a captain in the air force?"

"Yes, sir. I am. I'm also a certified pilot on the F-15 and F-16."

"You got a call sign?" Brandon asked.

"They call me 'Rebel' Randell. But we won't get into the reasons why."

"That's so cool," another boy said.

Then a little girl stepped up. Her name tag read Cassie. "Does your leg hurt?"

He looked down at the boot cast strapped on his lower leg. "Sometimes." He backed up, found a chair and sat down. "But not right now."

Livy moved in closer to Brady as if staking her claim. "Uncle Brady is going to marry me," the five-year-old announced.

"Is that true?" Sarah Ann, belonging to Brenna and Dylan, asked.

He looked up just as Lindsey arrived. Their gazes met, causing his pulse to race. "Yes, she's my best girl. She's going to take care of me when I'm old."

He stood and leaned toward Lindsey and whispered, "At least, it's the best offer I've had so far."

By ten-thirty that night Brady was parking at Lindsey's cabin. She didn't argue when he climbed out and came around to her side. Silently they walked down the slope to her cabin.

"So tonight you're going to let me walk you to the door?"

She stopped. "Not if your leg is bothering you."

"My leg is fine," he assured her.

Lindsey was nervous, more than any other time she'd gone out with a man. And she couldn't deny any longer this had been a date. They showed up at a family function together. And since they hadn't been able to keep their hands off each other, it would be wise to say a quick good-night and lock the door.

Right. She knew that wasn't going to happen, especially after having seen a different side to Brady tonight. How he'd interacted with the cousins and shown a softer side with the kids, patiently answering all their questions. So he wasn't the total tough guy he'd led her to believe.

How was she supposed to distance herself from this man?

After unlocking the door, she turned to face Brady, meeting his heated gaze. It was impossible. Silently she led him inside.

The room was illuminated by the dim light she'd left on. She saw his handsome face, along with the need reflected in his dark eyes.

Lindsey just wanted to drink in the beauty of the man. An inner strength and gentleness was underneath the cocky attitude.

The corner of his mouth twitched, then he lowered his head and brushed his lips across hers. The touch was featherlight, causing her to want more. Ache for more.

Then his mouth found its way to her ear, and she

shivered at the sensations he created. She gasped as he tugged on the hoop earring, causing other parts of her body to clench.

"You have to have the sexiest ears," he breathed. His hand moved upward and cupped her face. "But they've got nothing on your mouth." He dipped and took a nibble.

She gasped and made a moaning sound. Oh, how she wanted more, so much more.

He didn't disappoint her as his mouth closed over hers, angling his lips just perfectly to hers. Then his tongue slipped along the seam of her mouth, and she opened for him, welcomed him inside.

She clutched at his shirt, then slipped her arms around his waist, wanting to get closer to him. Brady helped things move on as he slid her coat off her shoulders, letting it drop to the floor, followed quickly by his. Next, it was her sweater that hit the ground, then his shirt disappeared.

He finally released her but never took his gaze from her. "I want you, Lindsey. But whether I stay or go is up to you."

She could turn him away. That would be for the best, but the feelings she felt for this man wouldn't let her deny herself this night. "Please, Brady, stay with me."

Brady gave a slight tug and they walked together into the bedroom. Once beside the large bed, he kissed her again and again. Then he sat down on the mattress and took off one boot and the cast. Lindsey removed her shoes, but when she started to take off her slacks, he stopped her and did it for her.

Standing there in her panties and bra, she enjoyed the hungry look in his eyes.

"You're so beautiful," he whispered and closed his mouth over hers until they both slipped onto the bed. Next came her bra.

She gave a moan as he circled one nipple with his tongue, causing the peak to harden. She arched her body and he opened his lips to take what she offered.

His easy hands moved over her warm skin, touching and stroking. It wasn't long before the rest of their clothes disappeared, and he lifted his body over hers. He paused as their gazes locked. She could see how tightly he was holding on to his self-control.

When it came to Brady Randell, she soon discovered she had no control.

CHAPTER SEVEN

LINDSEY woke with a start. She blinked to clear the fog from her head as the bright sunlight came through the window. She also heard the sound of the shower running. That was when the picture of a naked Brady Randell climbing into her bed and making love to her, again and again, flashed through her mind.

With a groan she flopped back on the pillow, clutching the blanket against her own nakedness. She rolled onto her side and inhaled the man's intoxicating scent, causing her to relive the pleasure he'd given her during their night together. She'd never experienced anything like it. Ever.

And she never would again. Not with this man.

She sat up. Her only alternative to correct this big error in judgment was to tell Brady the truth.

The bathroom door opened and the man in question came into the room. Oh, my. He was naked except for a towel wrapped around his waist. Beads of water still clung to his broad chest, then found their way down to his washboard-hard stomach.

With the last of her resolve, she forced her attention back to his face. Darn the man, he was grinning.

"Good morning, darlin'," he said as he limped to the bed, leaned down and planted a lingering kiss on her surprised mouth. "Yep, it's definitely starting out to be a good one, too."

"It's a late one." She glanced away. With a death grip on her blanket, Lindsey looked at the clock. Seven-thirty. "Oh, no, I need to be at the clinic by eight-thirty."

His gaze moved over her as a slow cocky smile crossed his tempting lips. "So I can't talk you into calling in late?"

She opened her mouth to answer, but no response came out. Good Lord, she was thinking about it. Was she crazy? "No!" she croaked. "I have scheduled appointments."

He looked disappointed. "Maybe later. Tonight?"

This had gone way too far, and she needed to tell him everything. "Yes, tonight. Now, I've got to get into the shower."

He nodded. "While you're showering, I'll fix breakfast."

He walked to where he'd dropped his jeans last night. She looked away as he slipped on his pants, then fastened his leg brace under the slit pant leg.

He grabbed his shirt and boot and headed for the door. He stopped and looked over his shoulder. "I could bring you coffee while you're in the shower."

She forced a smile. "No, thanks, I can wait."

"Well, holler if you need anything."

"I won't." She continued to sit there. "Now, would you mind?"

Brady wanted to hang around, just to see her blush some more. Lindsey wasn't dealing well with the morning-after routine. Not that he was a pro at this, either, but he wouldn't turn down an invitation to join her in another shower. But he knew that wasn't going to happen, so he wouldn't push it.

"I'll get coffee started."

He heard a murmured "thank you" as he walked out and closed the door. She wanted privacy. Okay, he'd give her that, he thought as he put on his sock and boot. He knew last night that Lindsey Stafford wasn't the type who usually brought men home. He liked that about her. Hell, he just plain liked her. A lot.

He made his way into the small kitchen, opened the coffee canister and scooped the correct amount into the coffeemaker, added water and turned it on.

Why was he still hanging around? That wasn't like him. He never wanted to give a woman the impression that this would lead to anything permanent. Over the years he'd tried relationships, but his career always came first. He couldn't blame women for not wanting to wait around for him.

Brady thought back to his own dad. He knew his parents' marriage wasn't perfect, but they loved each other, and their limited time together had been special to them. He'd always wondered if he'd find someone that he could love that much.

So far, no woman had held his interest beyond the casual stage. He'd decided long ago that a personal life would have to wait until he was a civilian again. He glanced down at his leg with the cast. That might come sooner than he wanted it to.

It had been a long few months since his accident. He glanced toward the bedroom door. Last night he hadn't thought about anything but being with Lindsey. She was different than any woman he'd known in the past. He liked her independence. She was self-assured in her work, and he especially liked how she cared about her patients. No doubt she could handle almost anything.

He took orange juice out of the refrigerator, noticing the shelves were bare. Toast would have to do, for now, but he owed Lindsey some decent food. Maybe he should have her over to his place for a change.

Whoa, he stopped. Was he crazy? His future was so uncertain, he couldn't begin to figure anything else out in his life.

Did he want this to go further? Suddenly he pictured the pretty redhead in bed last night and this morning. Oh, yeah, he wanted to see where this could lead, at least for a little while.

A knock sounded on the cabin door. Brady hesitated but decided that the Randells knew he'd taken Lindsey home last night. Besides, he was a little old to sneak out the back.

He opened the door to find a stranger wearing a sheepskin jacket. A black Stetson sat on his head. He had his back to him. At first he thought it was someone from the construction crew, then the man turned around.

Brady's breath caught as his gaze moved over the man's face, the square jaw and deep-set brown eyes. He had thick, steel-gray hair and a broad forehead, partially covered with a cowboy hat.

Damn, if he wasn't a dead ringer for his dad.

The older man frowned. "I'm sorry, I must have gotten the wrong cabin."

"Well, it all depends on who you're looking for," Brady said. "If it's a Randell, I'm your man, Uncle Jack."

The man's eyes narrowed, then he examined Brady closer. "You're Sam's boy?"

Brady couldn't believe it. Jack Randell had come back. "I'm one of them—Brady. Luke is the one you probably know about." What was he doing here after all these years? "If you're looking for your boys—"

"No! I'm not." He shook his head. "Actually, I'm looking for Lindsey Stafford's cabin."

Okay, he was confused now. Why would his uncle be looking for the vet?

Just then the bedroom door opened and Lindsey came rushing out, pulling on a sweater over her blouse. "I sure could use that coffee," she began. "But that's all I have time for." She finally glanced up and saw the two men at the door. She paled, then managed to say, "Jack. What are you doing here?"

Jack moved past Brady and into the cabin. "Funny, I came to ask you the same question."

Lindsey swallowed and tried to slow her heart rate. It didn't help. She stole a glance at Brady's confused look. She hadn't wanted him to find out this way.

She went to Jack. "I told you I was job hunting."

"Except you purposely left out the part about coming to San Angelo," Jack said. "If it wasn't for your friend, Kelly, I wouldn't have discovered what you're up to." He gave her a stern look. "Lin, we discussed this, and you agreed you'd stay out of it."

She took in his gaunt face. He'd lost weight. "I can't, Jack." She turned to Brady. "Brady, this is my stepfather, Jack Randell."

"Isn't this a kick? Your stepfather is my uncle. How about that for a coincidence."

Her voice softened. "I was going to tell you, I just couldn't find the right time."

His dark gaze grew hard. "Then I guess Uncle Jack showing up solved your problem." He looked at the older man. "You're legendary in these parts. And after all these years you come back. I'm curious if that's how you're going to greet your sons. You gonna just knock on the door. Surprise, here I am."

Jack shook his head. "I'm not going to disturb their lives. Lin and I are going back to Ft. Worth."

"No, Jack, you can't leave. You're here now, you've got to tell them."

Jack straightened. "Lindsey, I told you I'm not going there."

Brady grabbed his coat off the chair. "I'll let you two fight this out," he said as he headed for the door.

Lindsey went after him. "Brady, please." She grabbed his arm when he reached the porch. "You've got to let me explain."

"Why, so you can make an excuse about why you lied to everyone?"

"No, I didn't lie, everything I told you was true." She blinked at tears, biting back the words her stepfather refused to share with his family.

His eyes flashed. "So he sent you here to scout for sympathy."

That hurt her. "No. He wasn't going to contact his sons at all. This was all my idea." She rubbed the chill from her arms. "When I saw the ad for the veterinarian's position, I told myself I just wanted to meet one of Jack's boys. He'd talked about them for years, and Travis was doing the interview. I couldn't believe how much he looked like Jack. Then when he offered me the job, I found myself taking it."

She looked out at the scene of the incredibly beautiful valley. "Who wouldn't, Brady? I've heard stories about the Randell boys since Jack came to work on our ranch when I was ten years old." She didn't reveal that she'd always wanted to be part of that large family.

Brady jammed his hat on his head. "Then if you think he's so great, go back home with him. Believe me, when the brothers find out, there will be hell to pay."

She stiffened. "Then I'll pay because I'm not leaving here, not until Jack sees his sons." She fought her anger and tears. "And I plan to do everything I can to help him, and I'm not letting him lose—" she hesitated "—this chance to resolve things, not without a fight. So if you're going to run and tell the cousins, fine. I'll be ready for them."

Before she could leave, Brady grabbed her. "Dammit, Lindsey. Do you realize what kind of position you've put me in? I have nothing against Jack, but I owe some loyalty to my cousins. We're business partners."

She nodded, knowing Jack had more at stake. He could lose everything. "I know. And I owe my loyalty to the man I think of as my father. The man who helped raise me, who believed in me when I didn't believe in myself." She folded her arms over her chest. "Jack might have made a lot of mistakes when he was younger, but he's paid a heck of a price. He spent years in prison, lost his boys, his family." She looked Brady in the eye. "Mom and I did, too. I didn't lie about my childhood. Jack made us a family. Deep down, he's a good man, Brady. For God's sake, he's a Randell, too."

Brady cursed and paced the porch. "Hell, Lindsey, you're asking me to be his cheering section. I can't do it. I don't know how I can help you without causing a big family upheaval. And I'm not crazy enough to go against six brothers."

"Six brothers?"

Lindsey and Brady turned around to see Jack right behind them. "What are you talking about?"

Lindsey sighed and went to Jack. "It was something I learned just a few weeks ago." She took a breath. "You have three other sons, Jack. Jarred Trager, and twins Wyatt and Dylan Gentry. They've come here to live, too."

Jack paled and his eyes closed momentarily. "No wonder I'm so hated. Dammit, Lindsey, we're leaving."

She shook her head. "No, Jack, you can't. You've got to see this through."

"Well, I'm out of here." Brady started up the steps to where his car was parked.

Lindsey went after him. "Brady, wait. What are you going to do?"

He shook his head. "You tell me, Lindsey. What should I do? Just pretend I didn't see Jack Randell here?"

"No. But I just want a little time."

"Why? No amount of time will make this situation better."

"I know that. But I wasn't expecting Jack on my doorstep this morning." She couldn't blame him for feeling this way, especially after last night. She should have told him. "I'd already invited you back tonight, and I was going to tell you then."

"For another seduction so I wouldn't care about any of this deception?"

That hurt more than she wanted to admit to him. "You pursued me. You kept showing up at my door. I didn't set out for anything to happen between us." She could see by his steely look he didn't believe her. "Fine, do whatever you need to do, Brady. But I'm going to do any and everything I can to help Jack."

Lindsey turned around and made her way down the steps, hating that she'd allowed Brady Randell to get close to her. Well, never again. Ignoring Jack, she marched inside the cabin to the phone. She punched the number to the clinic and asked the receptionist to reschedule her morning appointments.

Jack had wandered back inside, too. "Give it up, Lindsey. Get packed and let's go home before anyone gets hurt."

"Stop it, Jack. I'm not letting you off the hook that easily. You're sick. Your sons are here." She released a breath. "You're the one who taught me never to give up, and now you want to. No. Forget it, I won't let you. I'm going to fight, Mom's going to fight, and you're going to fight, too." Tears filled her eyes. "We love you too much to let you go."

His eyes were sad. "You might just have to, Lin."

He came to her and hugged her close. She shut her eyes and allowed herself to feel his strength, his tenderness and the love she'd come to cherish. He'd saved her so many times over the years, she had to save him. She wasn't ready to let him go. No, not yet. She pulled back and wiped the tears away. "At the very least, Jack, you've got to see your sons."

He couldn't seem to say anything to that.

But she knew he wanted that, too. She punched out numbers on the phone.

"Lin, who are you calling?"

"I hope it's the one person who can help us. Hank Barrett."

About twenty minutes later Brady pulled up at the house. He parked the car and left the keys on the seat. He wasn't anxious to talk with Luke or Tess or anyone.

This way he didn't have to explain anything. Damn. The tranquil life he'd known since coming here was about to end. All hell was going to break loose, even if Jack Randell was smart enough to turn around and head for Ft. Worth. Brady knew he'd been here. He knew that Lindsey Stafford was Jack's stepdaughter.

Did Lindsey really come here on her own, or had Jack sent her to test out the waters? To see if his sons would be receptive to their father.

Brady shook his head. "It's none of my business." He didn't want it to be. He hadn't had Randells in his life growing up, but they'd gathered him into the fold even before he'd arrived here. He recalled waking up after surgery to see, not only Luke but Chance and Cade.

Brady thought back to Lindsey. Jack might have acted like a bastard to his sons, but he could see that father and daughter loved each other.

Brady climbed the single step to the porch. He sat down on the railing, recalling how Lindsey had responded to him last night. She'd held nothing back. After just a few weeks, he'd quickly learned she was that way about everything. She was fierce about her animals. He didn't doubt her love and loyalty for her family. For Jack.

"So you finally made it home."

Brady turned to see Luke coming up the path. "I didn't know I needed to check in."

"I'm not your keeper, Brady. I think it's great that you're getting along with Lindsey."

That was an understatement. "It's short-lived. We both know I'm going to be leaving soon."

Luke watched him. "You don't have to sound so anxious to go. We've kind of gotten used to having you around."

"Hell, you've only known me a few months."

"And you're my brother." He stared out at the corral. "Even though you're a pain in the butt sometimes, there's a bond between us. You feel it, too. We're family. We should be able to depend on each other."

That was Brady's problem. For so long he only depended on himself. He wasn't sure he could change— he thought of Lindsey—for anyone.

It took Hank an hour before he could get away to go and see Lindsey. She sounded anxious on the phone. He hoped she wasn't going to tell him she was leaving the valley. Well, he was going to do his darnedest to change her mind.

He parked his truck and climbed out, and that was when he spotted the black Ford crew cab pickup with the gold lettering for Stafford Horse Farm, Ft. Worth, Texas. So Lindsey's parents had come to visit her.

A strange feeling gnawed at his gut as he made his way to the cabin door. Then suddenly the pieces fit together. But before he could knock, the door opened and a large man stepped into view.

Deep-set brown eyes stared back at him, examining him closely. About sixty, with thick gray hair, he was wide-shouldered with an imposing barrel chest. He'd looked a lot older than his years, but Hank still had no trouble recognizing him. He'd seen those features every time he looked at his boys.

"Hello, Jack. I wondered if this day would ever come."

"Yeah, the rotten bastard came back."

"No, I was gonna say, I didn't think you had the... *cojones* to face your past. What changed your mind?"

Jack blinked. "Nothing. I came to get Lindsey. I don't want her exposed to my mess."

So his hunch had been right. "I thought I'd recognized the name when Lindsey mentioned it." He studied the man closely. "I'd heard you settled in the Dallas/Ft. Worth area after your release, and got a job at the Stafford Horse Farm. I take it Lindsey is your stepdaughter."

Lindsey appeared. "And proud of it. Hello, Hank."

She stepped back to allow him inside. Removing his hat, Hank followed Jack to the seating area by the fireplace. He took a seat across from Jack, watching the man. So different from the young, cocky, know-it-all guy who couldn't seem to stay home for his wife and boys. When he did, he ran his daddy's ranch into bankruptcy. Yet worst of all was when he'd been arrested for cattle rustling and was sent off to prison, leaving his three sons alone.

That was decades ago, but some scars never fade, especially for the kids left behind.

Lindsey came in carrying a tray with coffee. She set

it on the table. "Thank you, Lindsey." He picked up the steaming mug and took a sip. "Well, Jack. Tell me what this is all about."

Jack exchanged a look with Lindsey, but she spoke first. "Hank, Jack, didn't ever plan to come back here. My mom and I urged him many times, but he wouldn't do it."

"It was for the best," Jack said. "I knew the boys were settled with you, and you gave them a good life. I thank you for that Hank."

Hank nodded. "If that's true, why now?"

"It was because I came here." Lindsey exchanged another look with Jack. "I saw the ad for a vet and that Travis Randell was doing the interview, and I got curious. By the end of it I found I was agreeing to come here. I never meant to deceive anyone, but there wasn't a good time to blurt out who I was."

Jack interrupted. "I want her to return home and forget about this. I don't want any trouble, Hank. The boys are settled." He glanced away. "Lindsey tells me that I have three other sons."

Hank nodded. "Jarred Trager. Do you remember an Audrey Trager?"

Hank had to admit he got satisfaction seeing Jack uncomfortable. "Yes, I do."

"Then there's the twins, Wyatt and Dylan Gentry. Wyatt ended up buying your half of the Rocking R."

Hank could see more recognition and pain flash across Jack's face. "The ranch was in pretty bad shape when Wyatt got it, but it's a showcase now. Dylan showed up a few months later. He'd been badly injured by a bull while on the rodeo circuit."

"Dylan Gentry. He was world champion a few years back," Jack said.

Hank nodded again. "All the boys live around here now, they all married, happily."

Jack nearly jumped from his chair. "Stop. I have no right to know these things. I gave up those rights long ago."

Lindsey could see the pain in her stepfather's eyes. She wished he'd let her tell Hank about his illness. "Jack, you've always wanted to know how the boys were doing."

He swung around to his daughter. "It's worse knowing. I'm never going to be a part of their lives, or their children's lives." He drew a breath and calmed down. "I need to get back home to your mother."

Her mother? "You didn't tell Mom you came here?"

He shook his head. "I thought I could bring you home before she found out. She'd just worry."

"Jack, she's going to worry, anyway," Lindsey said, then turned to Hank. "The reason I came here was I was hoping his sons could help."

"Lindsey…" Jack sent her a warning look. "We're going home. I'm not going to see the boys."

"They're not boys anymore, Jack," Hank told him. "They're men and can make their own choices."

"Please, Jack," Lindsey pleaded. "You'll regret not talking to them before you leave."

She could see the pain in his face. "I can't mess up their lives again," he said. "I just can't, nothing is worth that."

Lindsey turned to Hank, fighting tears. "Please, make him understand this might be his chance to settle things."

"But it's a chance I'm not taking," Jack argued.

Hank held up his hand to stop them. "I think it's not up to you, Jack. It's your sons' decision."

CHAPTER EIGHT

BY the end of the day, Lindsey was exhausted. After the confrontation with Brady and Jack, the last thing she wanted to do was to take a call at the Rocking R Ranch. But after hearing Tess's concern about her colicky mare, Lindsey got there as soon as she could.

She wasn't ready to see Brady again, so she entered the barn on the corral side. How immature was that? As if she should care, since her job here would be coming to an end shortly. Just as soon as Hank talked to the brothers, Travis would ask her to leave.

She didn't want to think about how much she wanted to stay on. And if she were lucky enough to buy into a practice, this one would be perfect. She loved the area.

But she wouldn't leave Jack, not when he had to start treatment again. She wanted to be there for him and her mother.

Tess met her at the barn door. "Oh, Lindsey, thanks for coming so soon."

"Not a problem. How's Lady doing?"

Before Tess could answer, the horse whinnied. "As you can tell she's not good. She's been taking in a lot of water, and her respiration is rapid. We've had her off her feed all day." They headed out to the corral where Brandon and Luke were walking the animal.

Lindsey saw right away the animal was excited and thrashing as the teenager tried to keep her under control.

With a closer look, Lindsey was pretty sure what the problem was. "I think she's having intestinal spasms. Hear the gut noises?"

Both Luke and Tess nodded. "Yes."

"Spasmodic colic. Bring her into a stall," she told Luke.

Luke followed her orders, and led the mare inside. Once the examination was finished and an ailment was confirmed, Lindsey went to her bag, filled a syringe and injected the mare with an analgesic to relax the intestines. Slowly Lady began to calm.

She sent Brandon to her car for some supplies, mineral oil and lubricated tubing. With the others help, she administered a hearty dose of oil to the animal. Then they waited and let nature take its course. Soon after, the treatment began to take effect.

Nearly two hours later, a smelly and dirty Lindsey walked back to the car. Tess and Luke were still with Lady and Brandon had gone on home. The good thing about her fatigue was she hadn't had time to think about Jack waiting back at the cabin. She also knew he was going to try and convince her to come home with him.

Home. She wanted San Angelo to be her home, but knew that was pretty much impossible now.

Lindsey glanced up and paused, seeing a large figure in the shadows. Brady was leaning against her car. A shiver went through her. Why this man? Why did this man have to cause her to feel, to want, to desire?

He spoke first. "Is Lady all right?"

Lindsey continued toward the back of the SUV. "She is now." She set her case on the ground and opened the hatch. Brady came back and lifted the case to set it inside. "That's quite a fragrance you're wearing, Doc."

She knew she smelled, but the mare was better, and that was all that mattered. "It's one of the hazards of the job. That's what happens when you work around animals. Not a big deal, it'll wash out." She snapped her fingers. "That's right, you jet jockeys go for another kind of horsepower."

She was pushing him, but she didn't care. It was her only defense. She'd needed his support this morning when Jack showed up, and it hurt when he walked out. "Just so you know, I called Hank, and he talked with Jack. They're deciding what do." She slammed the hatch. "So don't worry, you're off the hook, Captain." She started for the driver's side, but he grabbed her arm to stop her.

"All right, so I didn't handle things well this morning." His gaze bore into her. "I'm new at dealing with family situations."

"You didn't handle anything, Brady, you walked away." She'd needed him, too. "After last night…" She hesitated then tried to pull away but he held tight.

"Dammit, Lindsey. It was a shock to find out my uncle is your stepfather."

"Okay, I blew it," she admitted. "But I never dreamed things would go so far, either. Just believe me when I say I was planning to tell you everything tonight."

He held her hand tighter. "Now that I've had a chance to think about it, I promise to listen to the whole story."

She needed to believe he was on her side, but couldn't yet. "Brady, I can't do this. I'm tired and dirty and I need to get back to the cabin. Jack is waiting."

He straightened. "That's it? You're just walking away?"

She didn't want to, but there wasn't any choice. "I can't worry about anything but Jack right now. He needs to see his sons, Brady. If only to close that door on his past mistakes. It's not going to be easy for any of us. You might have to choose sides." She didn't wait for an answer as she climbed into the car.

She couldn't bear to lose another man she loved.

Lindsey drove back to the cabin, praying for some good news. So far, she'd messed up royally when she only wanted to help.

Her biggest mistake was falling for Captain Brady Randell. No matter how things turned out for her job here, or for Jack, Brady was still going back to the air force. And he wasn't going to worry about the girl he left behind.

Great, she'd finally trusted a man and it was someone who didn't want the same things she did.

After parking behind the cabin, Lindsey walked down the slope. She didn't want Jack to see her worried, so she put on a smile as she walked inside. On the sofa Jack and her mother were in a tight embrace.

"Mom, you're here?"

Gail Stafford Randell pulled out of her husband's arms and stood. She wasn't much taller than her daughter, but her short hair was brown and she had large hazel eyes. At fifty-five, she looked trim in her dark slacks and teal sweater.

"Since I can't believe anything anyone in this family tells me, I decided I'd better come myself."

Lindsey felt tears rush to the surface. "I'm sorry, Mom. I never meant to make such a mess of everything."

"I know you didn't, honey. I'm still upset with Jack, though. He should have told me right away that the leukemia returned." She gave him an irritated look. "But, Lindsey, you should have let me in on your plan. I would have helped you."

Jack came up next to his wife. "And if I'd have faced my responsibilities years ago, we wouldn't be in this mess." His eyes narrowed. "But I'm telling you both right now, I won't coerce my sons. They don't owe me a thing. So they're not to know about my condition. Ever. You both have to promise me that you won't tell them."

Lindsey didn't want to, but she agreed. "What is Hank going to do?"

"He's talking to the boys tonight." He sighed. "So we'll know tomorrow if they decide to meet with me. I have no idea what to say to Chance, Cade and Travis. But even worse is Jarred, Wyatt and Dylan."

"We'll deal with it together." Gail's arm slipped around her husband's waist. The exchange of love Lindsey saw caused her chest to tighten. She couldn't help but envy what they shared.

Jack leaned down and kissed his wife. "That's because I have you, Gail. We'll get through this like we have everything else, as a family."

Her mother nodded. Tears filled her eyes as she rested her head against her husband's chest. Jack wrapped her in his strong arms.

Lindsey suddenly felt like a fifth wheel. She glanced

at her watch. "I need to get out of these smelly clothes and shower. I have another appointment."

"I bet you haven't eaten," her mother said.

Lindsey started for the bedroom. "Don't worry about me, I'll get something while I'm out. I'll probably be gone for hours. So please, you two take the bed."

"Honey, no," her mother said. "We can go to a hotel."

"No, I want you here. I'll just crash on the sofa when and if I get home."

She disappeared into her bedroom, then into the shower. Under the warm spray, she cried for her parents, for the Randells, for the years she'd taken for granted. Mostly she cried for herself, and the family she might lose.

Hank had summoned all six brothers to the house that night, but told Chance, Cade and Travis to come earlier. The four of them sat around the large kitchen table. The pine surface had many scars from the kids who'd eaten here for years. It was also the place where there had been many family discussions, punishments had been handed out and big announcements made. But never once in over twenty years, had he been able to tell his boys that their father had come home. Until tonight.

"I called all the brothers, but I wanted to talk to you three first."

The trio exchanged looks. "Come on, Hank, just tell us," Cade said.

"Okay. Jack is back."

He kept an eye on the three men he'd called his sons for over the last two decades. Their expressions were controlled, but he could see their underlying anger.

"What the hell does he want?" Cade finally asked. He'd always been the one to anger the fastest.

"Well, from what I learned today, he wants to see you boys," Hank told them. "Jack has been living outside Ft. Worth. He's been remarried for about a dozen years, and he breeds horses with his wife. You might have heard of the Stafford Breeding Farm."

"Wait a minute," Travis began. "Stafford. You can't mean to tell me that Lindsey Stafford is related to Jack?"

Hank nodded. "His stepdaughter. Lindsey told me she's wanted to tell you all who she was from the beginning, but never found the right time."

Travis spoke up. "So, she's trying to cozy up to us so Jack can come back into our lives?"

Hank raised a hand. "I don't think that's it. Lindsey swears she came here because she's always wanted to meet Jack's sons, and she found the opportunity when Travis went looking for Dr. Hillman's replacement."

"Does she think we're just going to welcome him back into the fold?" Chance said and shook his head. "I can't do it, Hank."

Travis and Cade murmured pretty much the same sentiment.

Hank hadn't hoped for much more. "Okay, but you know you're missing a good opportunity here. I mean, you always had questions you needed to ask him. If you refuse to see Jack, there might not be another chance."

Chance frowned. "I don't have much to say to him. When he got out of jail, he called and asked for money, which I gave him to stay out of our lives."

"And he's done that," Hank said. "I don't think he would be here if it weren't for Lindsey. She's the one who's campaigned for him to come back. She told me she was always curious about you three. Jack always talked about you."

"She should have told us who she was," Travis said.

"Would you have offered her the job?"

Travis folded his arms over his chest. "I'm not sure. Damn, she's a good vet. And everyone only has great things to say about her."

Cade spoke up. "How long would they, if they knew she was Jack's stepdaughter? People have long memories."

"And you boys have turned the name of Randell around to mean something good," Hank said. "There's a few old-timers who won't let go of what happened years ago, but you three have never listened to the talk. You've proven yourselves over and over again. You're your own men. And you're nothing like Jack. I'm so proud of you three, I can't even tell you."

The brothers sat up a little straighter.

"If it's any help," Hank went on, "Jack has turned his life around, too. The Stafford Horse Farm has a reputation as a top breeder in the area. Isn't it nice to know that he's doing well, too? That he's finally taken responsibility."

"I guess I wouldn't mind seeing him," Chance said, and looked at Hank.

The oldest of the three, Chance had been the one who'd tried to shield his brothers. He worked to keep them together, trying to be a man at fourteen. "I think I speak for all of us, that we haven't considered Jack our father for a long time," Chance said. "Not since we sat here that first time and you gave three scared kids a home."

Hank swallowed hard against the sudden emotion.

"Did we ever thank you?" Cade asked.

Hank nodded. "Every day when I watched you three grow into fine young men. A…a father couldn't be more proud."

Later that night a rainstorm moved into the area, dropping the temperature ten degrees. Brady was staying dry inside and fixing some soup. He'd planned his evening with supper and a strenuous workout, hoping to take the edge off his restlessness.

Now, if he could only stop the recurring thoughts of last night and Lindsey. How she'd felt in his arms, all soft and curvy. How her hands moved over his body, her mouth on his skin. He closed his eyes and his gut tightened as a renewed ache coursed through him.

A knock on the door brought him back to reality. He wiped his hand over his face. "You've got to pull it together," he warned himself as he walked across the room. He hoped the late-night caller wasn't his brother, wanting to go over business. He definitely wasn't in the mood.

Brady pulled open the door to tell Luke just that when he found Lindsey on the porch. She looked cold and miserable.

His heart soared. "Well, this is a switch. I'm usually pounding on your door."

She shivered. "My mother is at the cabin with Jack. I think they need to be alone." Those sad green eyes met his, then glanced away. "I didn't have anywhere else to go," she whispered.

He felt another tug inside his chest. "You do now."

In one swift motion he lifted her into his arms and over the threshold into the warm house.

"I know you're angry with me," she began, but he cut her off with a kiss so intense that when it finally ended they were both breathless.

"I'm getting over it." He brushed his mouth across hers again, loving the soft purring sounds she made.

"I didn't come here for this, Brady." She drew a breath. "Last night was a crazy mistake, for both of us. We don't need to repeat it."

"I'll go along with crazy, but what happened between us wasn't a mistake. It was damn incredible."

She pushed away from him. "Don't, Brady, I can't think straight when you say things like that. And I need to keep a clear head." She took another step back. "Along with a favor."

He shrugged. "Ask away."

"Let me hang out here for a while. Maybe sleep on your sofa."

His gaze searched her face. "You want to stay here?"

She nodded. "My mom and Jack need some time alone. I'm kind of the odd man out. I could go to a motel if it's a bother."

Lindsey Stafford definitely bothered him, in so many ways he'd lost count. He raised an eyebrow as the rain pounded against the roof. "How can I send you out in this? You hungry?"

She nodded and followed him into the kitchen. "I could eat."

"It's just tomato soup and grilled cheese."

"Some of my favorites," she said. "Let me help." She went to the hot griddle on the stove. A loaf of bread and cheese already sat on the counter. "How many sand-wiches would you like?"

"Two, but you don't have to cook them."

"I think I owe you a little kitchen time."

"If you insist." He went to the refrigerator and took out a jug of milk. He held it up. "This okay?"

Lindsey nodded and placed the buttered bread on the grill. She shouldn't have come here to Brady. She glanced at the handsome jet jockey with the day's growth of beard across his square jaw. He was too sexy for comfort. Those dark, deep-set eyes could pierce right through her resolve. Oh, yeah, she was in trouble. But she still didn't want to go anywhere else.

"Hey, stop thinking about it," Brady said, calling her back from her reverie. "Jack and the Randells will handle things."

"I can't help it," she told him. There was more riding on this visit than just patching up old times. "I never wanted to hurt anyone. They probably hate me now."

Brady came to her. "Stop. I've only known the Randells for a short time. If I've learned anything about them it's that they're fair. You didn't do anything to them. Their beef is with Jack. And from what I've heard they've got good reason." He kissed the end of her nose, then took the spatula from her and flipped the sand-wiches. "Now go sit down before you burn the food."

She huffed, unable to stop her smile. "I wasn't burning anything. They taste better with a dark, almost burnt crust."

"No. Golden brown is the only way." He scooped the cheese sandwiches off the grill. She carried the soup bowl then she glanced at the wall to see the calendar with the big red X marked at the tenth of the month.

She nodded to it. "What's that? D-day?"

"It's my next doctor's visit. Dr. Pahl is going to be the one who gives me the okay to shed this cast."

That was just a few days away. She looked across the table at Brady. She'd trusted him enough to share herself with him last night, body and soul. And she quickly discovered she wanted more time. "And if your leg has healed properly, do you go back to flying?"

He took a spoonful of soup. "I wish it was that easy. No, even with my doctor's okay, I still need the okay from a board of review to see if I'm fit to fly fighters again."

"You mean physically fit?"

"And mentally." He took a hearty bite of his sandwich. "No one wants any unstable pilots out there flying military aircraft."

"You aren't unstable." To herself she added, *A little stubborn, cocky and, oh, yeah, arrogant.*

"Thanks for the vote of confidence, but it's standard procedure that has to be followed."

"Well, I'm sure you're going to do fine," she said halfheartedly, knowing it was what Brady wanted, what he loved to do. She suddenly wasn't hungry anymore. "I guess both our lives will be changing soon."

His dark eyes locked with hers. "Why? You going somewhere?"

She shrugged. "This was only temporary. I doubt that I'm going to be staying here much longer." And she had to be back in Ft. Worth to help her mother with Jack.

"Doc, I doubt the Randells are going to send you away. You're too good at your job. Besides, I like the idea of coming back here and seeing you."

God, she was pathetic. She was actually thinking

about waiting around for a man who couldn't make her any promises.

"Dream on, fly boy, like I'll be holding my breath for your return," she lied.

Brady pinned her with a long, heated stare. She tried to draw in air, but it was difficult.

"Even as much as I might want to stay, Doc, I have a commitment to the air force."

"And I have a commitment to my career. I need to set up practice. My family is important to me. So I should go back to the Dallas/Ft. Worth area."

He scooted back his chair, reached for her and pulled her toward him.

She put up token resistance. "Brady, this isn't helping the situation." She went to him, anyway, allowing him to sit her on his lap.

He kissed her below the ear. "You know what, Doc?"

She gasped as a shiver went through her, and she wrapped her hands around his neck. "No, what?"

His mouth worked its way along her jaw. "When I look into your big, green eyes, you knock me out, you make me forget everything," he murmured. He raised his head, but his hands continued to move over her body, her bottom, up her back, drawing her in a tight embrace. "And when you're in my arms and I feel your body against mine, you make me forget everything but making love to you."

She tried to ignore the feelings, too. She pulled away and stood. It would be so easy to take the pleasure he offered, use it to help make her forget.

He came up behind her. "Lindsey?"

She turned around and saw the concern on his face.

"I'm sorry, Brady. I can't do this." She hesitated. "I should just leave." She tried to get past him, but he reached for her.

"The hell you are. Tell me what's going on."

"Just because I don't want to go to bed with you—"

"Hell, I've been shot down before, but I think there's something else going on here. Talk to me, Doc," he said in a husky voice as he reached for her.

She buried her face in his chest. God, it felt good just to lean on someone.

"It's Jack." She raised her head and looked him in the eye. "He's sick."

"How sick?"

"Very. That's the reason Mom and I tried to get him to come here and see his sons. He refused over and over. So when I saw the ad for the veterinarian…"

"You came here to try and pave the way for Jack," he finished for her.

She nodded. "He's not happy with me right now. And even though I'm here, he still made me swear not to tell Chance, Cade and Travis about it."

"Did he make you swear not to tell me?"

She looked at him. "No, but…"

He tugged her to the sofa and made her sit down beside him. "Come on, Lindsey, maybe I can help."

Brady might not love her, but she found she trusted him. She needed him to get through this. "Jack has leukemia."

He cursed and pulled her to him. It was like the floodgates opened as she began to tell him the four-year story. She shed tears as he held her. She fell asleep with the sound of his words in her ear, "Don't worry, Lindsey. It's going to be all right."

CHAPTER NINE

THE next morning, the rain was gone and the sun was shining. Brady ached to move and get the circulation back in his arm. He glanced down at Lindsey. Just as she'd been all night, she was curled up against him.

A strange feeling tightened his chest. She'd been carrying quite a burden around on those small shoulders of hers. And he felt privileged and humbled that she'd trusted him enough to share it with him.

She stirred in her sleep, shifting closer, and her breasts brushed against his chest. He bit down on his lip, feeling his body stir. She was killing him in more ways than one. He wanted Lindsey. He had from the moment he'd opened his eyes and seen her that first day on his porch. Keeping his hands off her during their evening together had been difficult, especially since they'd made love just the night before. He knew what it felt like to touch her, to feel her body react to the pleasure he'd given her.

He also knew that his longing hadn't stopped, his desire hadn't been quenched. He still wanted her more than ever. But right now she needed a friend more than a lover.

He grimaced. Friends with a woman? It had never been his style, but this pretty redhead had changed his mind about a lot of things. She'd pushed her way into his solitary life, making him rethink all other commitments.

Lindsey stirred once again. This time she blinked, then finally opened those incredible green eyes.

"Good morning, Doc."

With a gasp Lindsey sat up as she tried to regain some brain function. She'd spent the night with this man. She glanced down in relief to see they were both dressed and sharing the sofa in Brady's house. Memories flooded back and she remembered it all, especially the things she'd told him.

She brushed her hair away from her face. "I should get back to the cabin." She started to stand, but Brady stopped her.

"What is it about mornings that you're always so fired up to leave?" he asked. "Or are you just running out on me?"

She didn't want to acknowledge the closeness they'd shared last night. It had been far more intimate than anything physical that had taken place between them before. Now she'd shared her heart with this man.

"I just need to check on my parents."

"Okay, go call, but you better tell them you have plans this morning."

She raised an eyebrow. "I do?"

He nodded. Even with his hair mussed and his beard heavy, he was sexy as all get-out. "It's Wednesday and the clinic is closed this morning," he reminded her. "So how about playing hooky with me?"

She didn't like where this was leading. "Brady, I told you last night—"

"Doc, I'd like nothing better than a repeat of our night together." His voice turned husky. "Making love with you was incredible. But you're not ready."

She found herself blushing. Would she ever be ready for someone like Captain Brady Randell?

A lazy smile appeared on his handsome face. "So get sex off your mind, along with everything else, for a little while anyway. We're going horseback riding."

"You can ride?"

"I've been able to most of my life."

She frowned. "You know what I mean. With your bad leg."

"My leg is fine. I'm sure I can handle Dusty. Come on. I've been cooped up too long. I need to see some sky."

She got up so he could stand, too. "I'll still need to check my messages to see if there are any emergencies." She quickly went through about a half-dozen voice mails. One was from her mom. Lindsey returned the call and relieved her mother's concerns. She also heard about the meeting this morning between Jack and his sons. Once Lindsey hung up, Brady handed her a cup of coffee.

"Here, I think you need this."

"Thanks." She took the mug. "I also need a shower."

"I could use one, too. You go first, and I'll get in a short workout."

She nodded. "I carry a change of clothes in my car."

"I'll get them. You hit the shower." He headed for the door, but she stopped him.

"Brady, thank you for last night. You could have taken advantage of the situation."

He nodded. "Just so you know, Doc, I'm not always going to be a nice guy. Not when I want something. And I want you."

Hank wasn't sure how he was going to handle this meeting with Jack. He'd expected it years ago. Now the boys were adults, he wasn't even needed here, except that Chance asked him to come along.

Although the three sons had turned into six in the past few years, Chance, Cade and Travis were going to talk with Jack first. Jarred, Wyatt and Dylan would be arriving a little later.

Hank and Chance drove from the Circle B, and they were to meet Cade and Travis along the creek. As they got out of the truck, they saw the tall figure of Jack Randell already waiting under the trees.

They made their way down the slope beside Lindsey's cabin where they saw an attractive woman on the porch. He knew she must be Jack's wife and Lindsey's mother, Gail Stafford Randell. Hank nodded in greeting, not wanting to stop and visit at this time.

"Damn," Chance hissed and stopped on the path. "I didn't think it would be this hard."

"It's time to face him," Hank said.

"I know, let's get it over with." Chance nodded at the two riders coming in. "Here come Cade and Travis."

They rode in from the direction of Travis and Josie's house. Hank's chest tightened at the thought of his own daughter, Josie Gutierrez. He hadn't learned about her existence until she came to find him. He'd welcomed her with open arms, then after her marriage to Travis, he'd gifted her with Circle B acreage to build a home.

He'd divided the rest of the property between the boys he considered his sons, Chance, Cade and Travis.

They made their way to the edge of the creek, and to Jack. The two Randell men faced each other as if they were gunslingers from the Old West, instead of father and son. There was more silence as Cade and Travis dismounted and stood alongside their older brother. This was how it had been for years. You got one Randell brother, you got them all.

Chance spoke. "Well, we're here. What do you want?"

"Not a thing," Jack assured them, "except to see that y'all are doing okay."

"We're just fine. No thanks to you," Cade said.

Jack's gaze examined them all closely. "Yes, you boys have turned out fine." He took a breath. "I know this is a little late, but I want to apologize for not being around to raise you, and for causing you so many problems. I know it couldn't have been easy after I got sent away."

Hank could see the emotions all the men held in check.

"You're right," Travis said. "It wasn't easy, but as you can see, we survived. So it's a little late to be worrying about us now."

Jack nodded, looking pale under his tan, weathered skin. "Yes, you turned out fine. Thank you, Hank."

Hank nodded. "My pleasure."

Jack slipped off his hat and ran fingers through his hair. "There's one other thing I want to ask. You can be angry with me all you want, but don't take our problems out on Lindsey. She's innocent in all this. She only wanted to meet you all."

"She should have told us who she was," Travis said.

"Maybe, but I'm asking you to not hold that against her. She's a good veterinarian, and that's all that should matter."

Cade spoke up this time. "Or she might be a way for you to worm your way back into our lives."

Jack looked stricken. "If I'd wanted that I wouldn't have waited over twenty years." He put his hat on his head. "When a man gets to a certain age, he realizes he needs to make peace with his past. So I promise you that when I leave here today, it will be for the last time."

Brady had forgotten how good it felt to be in the saddle. The last time he'd ridden had been on his dad's ranch a few years back. He wasn't going to wait that long again.

He was on Dusty, and Lindsey was on Luke's roan gelding, Rebel. They were headed for the valley as the sun warmed up the early December air. Although they had worn jackets, he didn't doubt that they'd have them off before long.

"This was a great idea," Lindsey said.

"I come up with a few." He rested his hand against the saddle horn, giving his horse the lead.

"Your leg feeling okay?"

He grinned. "I told you, it's fine." In fact, he hadn't thought about it once. His concentration had been on Lindsey. She was smiling. He hadn't seen that in a while.

"I thought we'd head for the valley," Brady said. "It wouldn't hurt to check on the herd to see if they're okay."

"Good. It's been a few weeks since I've had the time to go by."

"You've had a few things going on, Doc." They rode side by side as they approached the rise. "Besides, there haven't been any incidents since the mare was shot. Maybe Hank's new security system is doing its job."

They started down toward the creek, looking for the mustangs. Instead, they saw a group of men.

Lindsey pulled up on the reins. "It's Jack. He's with Chance, Cade and Travis." She looked at Brady. "Maybe we should leave."

Brady watched the exchange between the men. His cousins were agitated. "They don't look happy."

"Oh, Brady, Jack's not as well as he's been pretending. And this stress isn't helping."

He reached for her hand and squeezed it. "Then tell his sons about their father's illness."

She shook her head. "Jack would never forgive me."

Brady wanted to shake them all. "Then the least we can do is even the odds. Come on, let's go stand with your father."

They made their way down and dismounted by the trees. Brady escorted Lindsey the rest of the way down to the group.

"Good morning, cousins," Brady said. "Hank, Uncle Jack."

"Lindsey, you shouldn't be here," Jack said.

"Maybe I should, since I'm the one who started all this." She looked at the three brothers. "It was never my intention to cause trouble."

"Jack's right, Lindsey," Cade said. "This doesn't concern you."

"Yes, it does," she corrected him. "Jack has been my father for the past dozen years. I love him." She fought tears. "Okay, he's made mistakes, but we all have."

"Lin, please." Jack went to her. "You don't need to defend me. We all know what took place all those years ago. I need to own up to it with my boys."

"Dammit, we're not your boys," Chance hissed.

Jack looked stricken. "I know. I gave up that privilege a long time ago."

There was only silence, until they heard the sound of the riders. It was Jarred, Wyatt and Dylan.

"We heard shots fired," Jarred called out.

Hank cursed. "Any ponies hit?"

Wyatt shook his head. "The herd scattered, but I think they're okay."

"Where did the shots come from?"

He pointed toward the west. "Same area as before."

"Well, this is going to stop today." Chance headed toward Lindsey. "You think I can borrow your horse?"

"Of course. I'll go to the cabin."

Chance went to Dusty and mounted up. His brothers did the same.

Brady was going to ride, too, but Hank stopped him. "Let's go in the truck. If the boys can't reach them, we'll be able to head them off."

Jack followed the group up toward the parking lot. "Mind if I go along?"

"I don't see why not," Hank told him.

Gail Stafford was waiting on the porch, but Jack only called to her that he'd be back soon.

"Take care of your mother," Jack said.

When Lindsey started to argue, Brady reached for

her. "Look, it'll be better if you stay here. Then I don't have to worry about you, too."

She nodded. "Just watch out for Jack."

"Sure." He leaned down and gave her a quick kiss. "We'll be back soon." He tipped his hat to Gail, then hurried to Hank's truck.

"You drive, Brady," Hank insisted, then headed for the passenger side while Jack climbed in the back door.

Brady started the engine and headed toward the highway, all the time aware of the danger. "Maybe you should call the sheriff, Hank."

Hank pulled out his cell phone. "A lot of good it'll do us."

"It's a precaution. If anything happens today, we want it on record that we called the authorities."

Jack spoke up from the backseat. "I take it these guys have taken potshots at the ponies before."

"We've had two wounded in the past few months. Thanks to Lindsey, the little buckskin mare recovered."

"That's my girl," Jack said proudly.

Hank continued to fill him in as Brady turned off the highway. Jack climbed out to open the gate, then returned to the truck.

"The lock's been busted," he told them.

Hank's fist hit the dashboard. "I'll get these guys if it's the last thing I do. And I might just tan their hides before I turn them over to the sheriff."

"I might just hold them down for you." Brady drove along the bumpy dirt road, then turned at the fork. After another half mile, he pulled off and parked. They all climbed out, then Hank took two rifles off the rack in the back window of the truck.

"I'm not going in without backup," he said.

Brady called Chance to learn their location, then he silently walked toward the spot where he and Lindsey had found the camp once before. He heard voices, and used a hand signal to alert Hank and Jack that he was going closer.

The thick mesquite bushes were great cover so he could peer at the intruders. Four teenage boys were sitting on the downed logs, drinking.

Brady returned. "There's four of them," he said. "Teenagers. They have two rifles, but it gets worse. They're passing around a fifth of whiskey."

"Somebody raided their daddy's liquor cabinet," Jack said.

"Their parents aren't going to be happy to have to bail them out of jail, either," Hank added. "I'm pressing charges."

Brady wasn't crazy about dealing with drunk kids, especially holding firearms. He pulled out his phone and called the sheriff again, telling him what they'd found.

Closing his phone, he reported, "A deputy is on his way."

"I'm not letting them get away. So it looks like we're on our own," Hank said.

Brady looked at Jack, noticing his rapid breathing and pale complexion. "Are you okay?"

Jack brushed off the concern. "Sure, I'm fine. I'll hang back in case one of them tries to run."

They circled the area, then Hank showed himself first. He cocked his rifle and pointed it. "Okay, boys, the party's over."

The teenagers jumped up, shouting curses. One tall, thin boy boldly stepped forward. "It's only an old man."

"Well this old man is going to make your life miserable." Hank waved the rifle. "Now, move away from the weapons. We don't want anyone to get hurt."

"We don't have to listen to you," the same kid mouthed off.

"Look, I'm the one holding the rifle on you. And you're trespassing on my land, shooting at defenseless animals. Wild mustangs. So I'd suggest you keep your mouth shut. Now, move." He waved the barrel of the rifle to show the direction.

Brady came into view. "I'd do as he says if I were you."

They reluctantly walked away from their whiskey and rifles. "My daddy isn't gonna like what you done," one of the boys said as he swayed on his feet.

"If your daddy's smart, he'll whip your butt for this stunt."

The boy cursed. "Old man, you're gonna be sorry. My daddy is important in this town."

Brady could see one of the smaller kids looking panicky. Then suddenly the boy took off running. "Dammit." He looked at the other kids. "Don't even think about it."

Suddenly they heard the boy cry out. Brady went to see that Jack had tackled the kid. Brady smiled. "Hey, Jack, you need some help?"

"No, I got him."

Brady turned back to the other boys to see if they'd lost their attitudes.

"What are you going to do to us?" the kid asked.

"Nothing. We're turning you over to the sheriff."

Just then Chance came riding in. "Good, you got 'em." He climbed down as Jack brought in the other boy.

Chance took the rope off his saddle and began tying the boys' hands.

Brady gave his rifle to Cade when he arrived, then went to help Jack. The man was leaning against the kid's truck. They tied the teenager's hands with rope from the truck bed. Brady directed him toward Chance, then came back to Jack.

"You don't look so good," he said, seeing the blood drain from Jack's face. "I think we should head back."

"I wouldn't mind that." He pushed himself off the truck, swayed, then collapsed.

Jack Randell was unconscious before he hit the ground.

CHAPTER TEN

AN HOUR later, trying to control her panic, Lindsey and her mother hurried through the hospital doors and upstairs to the third floor. Brady had called about Jack's collapse and instructed her where to come, but she had no idea what condition her stepfather was in.

All the way up the elevator, she couldn't help but blame herself for this mess. If only she hadn't come here....

"Stop trying to second-guess yourself, Lindsey," her mother said. "Jack needed to come back here and see his boys."

"But I could have handled things differently." She bit back the tears. "And if Chance, Cade and Travis knew about Dad's condition, they could help him."

Her mother gripped her hand. "And we both know Jack would never ask them."

The doors opened and they went to the desk to get information. She looked around for Brady.

Not only Brady, but every one of Jack's sons were in the waiting area. Chance, Cade and Travis stood by the window, and talking with Brady were Jarred, Wyatt and Dylan. When Brady saw her, she felt her chest tighten. She needed him. He didn't disappoint her as he came to her.

He hugged her close. It felt so good, she never wanted to leave the safety of his arms. Finally she raised her head. "Where's my dad?"

"He's down the hall. Dr. Hartley is with him." He looked at her mother. "Mrs. Randell, I'm Brady Randell. I'm sorry about your husband. We got him here as soon as possible."

"Thank you." Gail nodded, fighting tears. "He's been really sick. We need to get him back home."

Before Brady could speak, the doctor came out of the room down the hall. Gail Randell went to him, and Lindsey followed her. "Dr. Hartley, I'm Gail Randell, how is my husband?"

The gray-haired specialist frowned. "He's a sick man, Mrs. Randell. Thanks to the information your daughter gave us over the phone, I've been in touch with his oncologist in Ft. Worth." He sighed. "I don't need to tell you Mr. Randell's condition is serious."

Gail shook her head.

"The recurrence of his leukemia and the failure of all aggressive treatments leaves a bone marrow transplant as his only option," the doctor stressed. "He's on the national donor list, so there isn't much else we can do for him."

"Is…is he going to die?" her mother asked.

Dr. Hartley paused, not needing to say the words. Then he glanced at the men in the waiting area. "Unless you can find a relative to be a donor."

Lindsey felt her mother's trembling hand. "Can I see him?"

With his nod, Gail released her daughter, then went with the doctor. Lindsey turned around to find Brady standing behind her. "Thank you for all your help."

"Hell, I didn't do anything. Not yet, anyway." He went down the hall to Jack's room. He caught Dr. Hartley just outside. "Doctor, I'm Jack Randell's nephew. Where do I go to be tested as a donor?"

Lindsey caught up to hear his words. Her chest tightened. Brady hadn't hesitated to give her father this chance for survive. At that moment she couldn't love him more. "Oh, Brady."

"It's okay, Lindsey." He pulled her close. "We're not giving up yet."

"Give up what?" Chance asked as he showed up, followed by his brothers. "What's wrong with Jack?"

With a reassuring glance from Brady, Lindsey announced, "Jack has acute lymphocytic leukemia. He needs a bone marrow transplant."

"I'm getting tested." Brady held Lindsey tighter as he watched his cousins absorb the information.

"So that's what he came back for?" Cade asked.

Brady stiffened. "Will you get rid of the attitude? This isn't the time to drag up the past. Whatever you think about your father, let it go. Jack could be dying."

He glanced at the group of Randell brothers who circled him and Lindsey. "Even with the good, the bad and the ugly, your stepsister loves that man in there." He pointed toward Jack's room. "The same man who made all those mistakes years ago. But I think he's redeemed himself a little because of how hard he's worked and the accomplishments he's made the past twenty years."

Brady started to walk away. "Oh, and the reason

Jack came here was to bring his daughter back to Ft. Worth. He didn't want her involved in his mess. But Lindsey convinced him to at least see his sons. All he wanted from you boys was to make peace."

He turned away. "Okay, Doctor, show me where I need to go." He kissed Lindsey, promised to be back, then went off with the doctor. By the time he got to the elevators, he discovered the other Randells had followed him. "What now?"

"Maybe we want to be tested, too," Travis said. "We're probably a better match than you, anyway." His gaze narrowed. "You got a problem with that?"

"None whatsoever." Brady only prayed that someone was a match for Jack.

A few hours later, when Brady got back upstairs, he saw his brother, Luke, and suddenly he felt pretty lucky to have him there.

"Hey, I hear it's been a pretty busy morning."

"Yeah. Lindsey's having a tough time. We're all waiting to see if any of us are a match as a marrow donor."

"I hear you started things off."

Brady shrugged. "I couldn't just stand by and not do anything." He sighed. "I look at Lindsey and can see how much she loves him." He caught his brother's gaze. "The man had to do something right to gain her loyalty."

"Lindsey's pretty special. You care about her, too."

"Yeah, but that doesn't mean it's headed anywhere."

Luke smiled. "Not long ago I thought the same thing about Tess."

In the waiting room, Lindsey couldn't believe she was sitting with her stepbrothers. They were actually carrying on a conversation, wanting to know about the years with Jack.

"I wasn't exactly a model teenager," she told them.

"That makes me happy," Chance said, "knowing you gave Jack a rough time. I love payback."

"Oh, I did that and more. I ran away more times than I could count." She looked over at Jarred, Wyatt and Dylan. They had stayed in the background most of the day, although they volunteered to be tested as donors along with the other brothers. "About the age of fifteen I realized he wasn't going to give up on me."

"He never would, either."

Lindsey swung around to see her mother had joined them. When the men started to stand, she motioned for them to stay seated.

"How is Jack?" Lindsey asked.

"He's resting comfortably." She blew out a breath. "Jack asked to see Jarred, Wyatt and Dylan." She raised a hand. "But he'll understand if you don't want to see him."

The three glanced at each other. "I guess it's about time we met him," Jarred said as he stood. The others did the same and they all went off to the room.

Gail turned back to the group and sat down in one of the vacant chairs. "I've wanted to meet you all for so long." She put on a smile. "Jack has spoken of you boys nearly every day since we met. When he first came to the ranch, he'd just been released from prison. He needed a job and I needed help with our rundown farm. The only place I had for him to stay was the barn."

She blinked rapidly. "He worked from sunup to sundown, doing needed repairs and working with the four horses that I was able to hang on to.

"When Jack finally began to talk, it all just poured out of him. That's how I learned about you boys. He had pictures, too. Of course, you were all a lot younger then." She scanned the row of large, strapping men. She nodded at Chance. "You're Chance. Your hair is the lightest sandy brown, and your eyes, too." She continued her search. "Cade, you're the tallest. And Travis, you're the baby of the family."

"Not any longer," he said. "Wyatt and Dylan are."

"If you take away nothing else, just know Jack was proud of all of you, although he knew he had nothing to do with it. He was just happy that you had someone like Mr. Barrett to take care of you."

"Yeah, we were lucky," Travis said. "Hank was the father that Jack never could be."

Gail nodded. "Just because he gave you up doesn't mean that you aren't in his heart."

Lindsey glanced around at the men, seeing the raw emotion in their eyes, and the way their throats worked as they swallowed back more feelings than they could admit.

"I can't thank you all enough for offering Jack this chance." She brushed away a tear and smiled. "Even if it doesn't work out, Lindsey and I will never forget what you've done."

The room was silent. Then came sound of footsteps as Dr. Hartley made his way to the group.

"Mrs. Randell. It looks like we have a donor match."

There was a pause, then Cade said, "Don't keep us in suspense, Doctor. Who is it?"

The doctor scanned the three remaining Randell brothers. "It's Chance."

* * *

The following Monday, Brady sat in Dr. Pahl's office, waiting anxiously for the news as the orthopedic surgeon looked over the X rays and MRI again.

"Your fracture has healed nicely," he said. "And there's no permanent damage to the muscle or tendon." The young doctor sat down on the front edge of his desk. "In other words, Captain, I'm releasing you and sending you back to active duty."

Brady had wanted this for months, but now that it was actually happening, it seemed too soon. "That's great news."

The doctor gave a curt nod. "By this time next week you'll be back at your home base in Utah."

Brady wanted to be happy, but he knew he had a way to go before he was able to climb back into the cockpit. "Thank you, Doctor. You'll never know how much this means to me." He stood and shook the doctor's hand.

"You're welcome, Captain. I'll send all your medical records to your commanding officer. Good luck."

Brady walked out of the office, without his cast for the first time in months. A smile broke out as he took off in a near run through the parking lot. He started the car and pulled out into the street to go back to the ranch.

Suddenly it seemed a lifetime ago since he'd been at Hill AFB. It had been. A long four months since he'd been to his apartment just off the base. He'd been deployed overseas for a few weeks when the accident happened and they flew him back to the States.

To San Angelo. To his family. Although they had crowded him sometimes, he'd found he kind of liked being part of the craziness. The family get-togethers. It was the first time he'd spent Thanksgiving with relatives.

Then there was Lindsey. Being with her had been like nothing else he'd experienced with a woman. Yet, since that night in the hospital, he hadn't seen or heard from her. Mostly it was his fault. He knew he'd be leaving soon, and she needed to be with her family. He'd called her a few times, but got her voice mail. He'd never left any messages.

Lindsey had her family here, and she was busy with the vet practice. Now more than ever, their lives were starting to run in different directions.

In a few days she'd return to Ft. Worth for Jack's procedure. Since Chance had agreed to be the marrow donor, they were busy doing the final prep for the surgery. And by then Brady would be on his way to Utah and his squadron.

Brady decided not to push his attentions on Lindsey. He needed his own space, too. All he'd done was think, and it had only been about Lindsey. She'd become more important to him than he'd thought possible. She was the first person he wanted to share his news with. He passed the ranch and headed for the cabin. He didn't know what he was going to say, only that he needed to see her.

Lindsey stacked her suitcases by the door and glanced around the cabin that had been her home for the past few months. A tightness constricted her chest, and she fought tears. She'd come to think of the place as hers. She'd never forget the time she'd spent here with Brady. The night they'd made love. Never before had she given herself so completely to a man, body and soul...and heart.

She closed her eyes, reliving his touch, each caress and each kiss. How she prayed it would never end. During those hours in his arms, she'd fallen in love with him. Then she woke up the next morning knowing she had to let him go. He'd be returning to the air force, and she was headed back home with her parents.

No more delays, either. She opened the door and stepped out onto the porch, but stopped suddenly when she ran into a hard body.

"Oh," she gasped, and looked up. "Brady?"

He smiled, but his hands remained on her waist. "Hi, Doc. Catch you at a bad time?"

She wasn't sure she could answer. It had been four days since she'd seen him. She shook her head. "Do you need something?"

"I just wanted to see you." He kept coming toward her until she backed through the door. "I missed you."

I've missed you, too, she cried silently. "I pretty much stayed at the hospital. Mom needed me."

He played with the hat in his hand. "That's understandable. Is everything going okay with the upcoming marrow transplant?"

She nodded. "Chance is on his way to Ft. Worth." She stole a glance at him. "I never got to thank you for helping us, for being the first to volunteer to be a donor."

He shrugged. "Not a big deal. I knew my cousins would step up."

"Well, I'll never forget it," she told him.

He studied her for a long time. "Are you coming back here after the procedure? I hear there's a permanent position to fill."

It was hard to answer. She wanted to, but not when

Brady would be coming back and forth, too. "Hank and Dr. Hillman have both talked to me about it." She shook her head, unable to tell him the real reason, that she didn't want to run into him. "I don't think it's such a good idea, especially with my relationship to Jack."

"I doubt the brothers are the type to hold a grudge against you."

"It's still best I stay close to home. Jack and Mom need me right now. At least for a few months."

"I'm sure they'll want you to go ahead with your own career."

"Whether that's true or not, my family will always come first. I should find a job around Ft. Worth." She glanced down to notice he was missing his cast. "Oh, Brady, you went to the doctor?"

He nodded. "He released me this morning. My leg is healed perfectly. You're the first person I've told."

She didn't want to read anything into his comment. "When do you go back?"

"I need to report to my base Monday morning."

Her heart ached, but she put on a smile. "That's wonderful news. You can fly again."

He raised an eyebrow. "That's not confirmed yet, Doc. But I'll know soon. They're reviewing my accident right now."

"You'll get back into the cockpit. I have complete confidence that "Rebel" will be flying once again. You'll be back to doing what you love."

He hesitated. "I'm not so sure anymore, Doc. A lot of things have changed in the past few months…since the accident. Since you." His gaze went to hers in a heated look. "I came to realize how my career was all I had."

"But you have a brother now and cousins." She smiled. "And a cute little niece who adores you."

He shrugged. "Yeah, and I ran headlong into a beautiful redheaded vet who put me in my place."

She shrugged. "I didn't want you to get bored while your leg was healing. It's a known fact fighter pilots are a cocky lot."

"I've heard more colorful words used to describe me. How did you manage to put up with me?"

It was easy, she whispered to herself. "By humbling you to do my dirty work."

"You have an incredible way with animals. Following you around was fascinating."

"There are easier ways to kill time."

At that he reached for her and pulled her into a tight embrace. "Doc, believe me, killing time was the last thing on my mind. Those nights I spent with you meant something. More than you'll ever know. At least if this is going to end, can't we be honest with each other?"

She didn't want honesty. "Why? What good would it do, Brady? Sorry. I'm a big girl. I've accepted that you're leaving." She was lying big-time.

He nodded. "Dammit, Lindsey. I have a commitment to the air force."

"And I respect you for that."

"Hell, Doc, I wish you didn't. You don't think I want more for us? I want you so bad, I want to kidnap you and steal you away with me." His mouth came down on hers in a bruising kiss, then it gentled as his arms cradled her against him.

His hard body pressed to hers, creating an unbearable need only Brady could fill. She whimpered softly and wrapped her hands around his neck, arching her body into his, wanting to grasp this moment and this feeling forever.

"Brady," she breathed, and pulled back. "We can't keep doing this." She loved him so much it was killing her.

He finally stepped back. His dark eyes narrowed, as his hands cupped her face. "I could get lost in you so easily. Your eyes mesmerize me, your body tempts me. Ah, hell, Doc, you make me forget everything."

"Problem is, Brady, we can't forget our obligations."

His gaze locked with hers. "I wish…I wish we had more time. Wish things could be different."

She stepped back, putting more space between them. "No, Brady. We always knew it could come to this point. You have a military career. You're a Fighting Falcon pilot. You have to be so proud of that. I am."

He nodded. "I'm proud of you, too, Doc. You have a pretty good career started yourself, wherever you decide to practice. But I have to say I wish you were coming back here. I like to think about you with the mustangs. That little buckskin mare wouldn't be here if you hadn't nursed her back."

"And you helped catch the guys who were shooting at them." She paused, her voice grew soft. This was goodbye and they both knew it. "I only wish the best for you, too, Captain." She turned away to catch her breath, then looked back at him. Big mistake. She straightened defensively. "Look, Brady, I have an appointment I have to get to. Then I'll be leaving tomorrow."

He continued to stare at her. "So this is it? We just go our separate ways?"

"There doesn't seem to be any choice."

* * *

The following twenty-four hours seemed endless. Lindsey was gone. Brady was leaving the next day, so he took advantage of the little time he had left. He ignored Luke's request to see the progress of the Golden Meadow project. He trusted his brother's expertise. Instead he took refuge in horseback riding. He'd only had one other opportunity, and that had been with Lindsey. Oh, God, he wished now he could have more time with her.

Brady pulled on Dusty's reins as they arrived at the creek that edged the valley. Maybe he'd come here to remember his time with Lindsey, or maybe it was to say goodbye to what they'd shared here. There was no telling when he'd be back.

His commanding officer had called earlier, telling him of the review board meeting. That they would have the results by the time he returned to the base. That would be 1600 hours on Monday when he was to report to the base.

Then his thoughts turned back to Lindsey. Their last kiss, their bad goodbye. The longing he'd felt since she'd left the valley. She just tore out his heart and walked away. He took a breath. Oh, damn. At this moment, never seeing her again seemed harder than anything. Now he realized how his parents must have felt whenever they were separated. How does a marriage survive when you're apart so much?

He glanced out at the herd of mustangs and saw the buckskin mare Lindsey had treated. She belonged here, working with the ponies, making sure they were healthy and safe.

Everything she loved was here.

When Brady heard his name called out, he turned around and saw his brother riding toward him in the golf cart.

"Hey, you're a hard guy to track down."

"I've been around. Something wrong?"

Luke smiled. "No, I'd say everything is going right. Joy called from Ft. Worth. The bone marrow transplant is scheduled for Tuesday morning. I thought you'd want to know."

Brady closed his eyes momentarily. Lindsey had to be happy, but scared, too. "Thanks."

"I was kind of surprised you didn't go to be with her."

"I don't think she needed me around."

Luke shrugged. "Funny, it didn't seem that way to me. You two seemed pretty tight these past few weeks."

"Things change," Brady said. "Doc decided to return to Ft. Worth, and I have to go back to my squadron."

His older brother frowned. "You're not worried about being cleared to fly again are you?"

"No. It's just a lot of things are different now."

Luke smiled. "A woman always changes things. If it's the right woman, it's all good."

"What if I'm not ready for *that* woman?"

Luke grinned this time. "Are we ever really ready? But take it from me, having Tess in my life makes it worthwhile. You can lose everything and it doesn't matter, not when you know she loves you."

Brady suddenly realized that he wanted Lindsey with him. "How can I ask Lindsey to give up everything she's worked for and follow me around from base to base?"

"I don't know." Luke shrugged. "But I think you need to give her the opportunity to decide."

Brady blew out a breath. "Doesn't seem fair."

Luke patted his brother on the back. "Cousin Chance once told me that Randell men seem to fall hard for their women. And they love forever.

"So ask yourself, brother, do you want Lindsey forever?"

CHAPTER ELEVEN

THE next afternoon Lindsey stood in the hospital room watching Jack sleep. He wore a surgical mask over the lower half of his face, to keep him as germ free as possible. It was worth the inconvenience before and after the procedure. The important thing was after the marrow transplant, she knew Jack was going to get better. Tomorrow would be a long day for all of them. Her mother was back at the hotel resting, too.

Lindsey looked out the window at the cold December day. So many times in the last week she'd thanked God for this miracle. Not only for the bone marrow, but the chance Jack had gotten to see his sons again. She doubted the Randell brothers would ever take him back as their father, but they'd all moved on enough from the past to want to help.

She felt the raw emotions surface again and fought them. She needed to be strong to handle the next few days. But not everything was so easy to put aside or forget. She thought about Brady. He'd probably gone back to Utah by now. Over the past few days, Tess had called several times to keep her informed, but she hadn't heard anything about Brady's review board. Not that Lindsey had asked.

"You're looking awfully worried." Jack's voice broke through her reverie. "Is there something else the doctor's told you?"

"No. Just that you're going to be around a long time." She kept a safe distance. "You should be resting."

"Seems that's all I've been doing," he told her. "Speaking of which, aren't you tired of hanging around my room?"

"Someone has to make sure you behave yourself."

He ran a hand over his gray hair. "I've been too weak to do anything else." He glanced around. "Please, tell me your mother left to get some rest."

"Yes, about an hour ago."

"Then I want you to go, too." He raised a hand when she started to argue. "Please, Lin, you need to get out of here for a while."

She bit down on her lip. "Are you trying to get rid of me."

"Oh, no, darlin'." He held out a hand and she came to him. "I know this has been hard on you and your mother, but it's going to be okay."

"We don't want to lose you."

"You won't. We have our miracle. A second chance." He hugged her close as her tears fell freely. Finally he spoke again. "I have a feeling this might be about something else entirely. Maybe a certain air force captain."

She pulled herself together and stood. "It doesn't matter. He's gone back to the base. I'm not going to run after him, either. Not when he didn't have a problem leaving me."

Jack pulled the surgical mask down to make a point. "He's in the air force, Lin. He doesn't have a choice."

She raised a hand. "I know, I know. The military comes first. I just wanted him to care enough about me to ask if I want to share that part of his life."

"There's no doubt Brady cares for you, Lin, but he has commitments. You've got to give him time to work through them." Jack smiled. "You're a lot like your mother. Believe me, you won't be easy for him to forget."

She wanted to believe him, but Brady was still gone. And she was here…alone.

"You're tired, honey. You need to get some rest, too. You've spent all your time helping me." He gripped her hand. "How can I thank you for bringing me together with my boys? Starting tomorrow, I'm going to take charge of this family again. What can I do to help you?"

She loved him so much. "Just stay around a long, long time."

He grinned. "I'll do my darnedest."

"Good." She smiled.

Suddenly a familiar figure appeared at the glass partition. It was Brady, looking tall and handsome in his air force blue dress uniform, his cap tucked under his arm. His once-shaggy black hair was now cut military short.

Her heart accelerated more as she glanced up at the man's face, and familiar brown eyes stared back at her.

"Hi, Doc," he said from the doorway. "Your mother told me you were visiting your dad." He turned to the bed. "Hello, sir. I hope I'm not disturbing you."

Jack sat straighter in the bed and replaced his mask. "No, of course not. I wish I could invite you in, but there are rules."

Brady smiled. "Not a problem, sir. Wouldn't want to do anything to upset tomorrow's procedure."

"That might not be taking place if you hadn't started things. I'm grateful to you for offering to be a donor."

"I'm glad everything worked out."

Lindsey couldn't believe he'd shown up here. "Brady, I thought you were going back to your base."

He checked his watch. "I am. I just took a detour. My connecting flight leaves in a few hours. But I wanted to see how Jack and you were doing."

She felt herself blush.

Her father spoke. "I'm doing fine, Brady, even better after tomorrow."

"I wish you only the best, sir."

"And I appreciate you coming by," Jack said. "We never got much of a chance to talk. Sam and I were close growing up, but things changed over the years. I believe your father would be happy his sons are back at the Rocking R." He smiled. "I hope if you ever get back to Ft. Worth, you'll stop in and see us. I'll tell you some great stories about your daddy."

Brady nodded. "I'd like that, sir. Right now, I have some things to straighten out with my career." He turned to Lindsey. "And lately things have gotten more complicated."

Lindsey could feel the heat of his gaze, making her uncomfortable. "Dad, I think I will go back to the hotel."

Brady stepped in. "Lindsey, could I talk with you?"

She sighed. "I don't think there's anything to say."

He blocked the doorway. "Please, let me walk you out."

She nodded, then glanced at her stepfather. "Now, you better get some rest, too. Bye, Jack."

Brady said his goodbye, too, and allowed Lindsey out into the corridor, then they walked to the elevators.

Her chest tightened at the thought of talking with him. "What are you really doing here, Brady? We already said everything."

"You think we could find somewhere to talk?" He checked his watch. "Maybe I can walk you to your car. You look dead on your feet."

"Just what every woman wants to hear."

He took a step closer. "I didn't mean it that way. You're a beautiful woman, Lindsey. Missing some sleep could never take that away." He took her by the arm and walked her to the elevator. Silently they rode down to the first floor, then out the front doors and across to the parking structure.

Lindsey walked fast, aching to get this over. Soon they were next to her SUV.

She drew a calming breath. "Why are you really here, Brady?"

"I wanted to make sure you were okay. I couldn't leave things the way they were, Doc. Without letting you know what you mean to me."

Before she could speak, his mouth closed over hers in a tender kiss that only made her want more. More than he could give her.

He pulled back. "I told myself I wouldn't do that." Frowning, he cursed. "But I can't help remembering how you felt in my arms." He paced back and forth. The sound of his shoes echoed in the deserted structure. Then suddenly he stopped in front of her. "I never expected to find someone like you. Someone who made it so damn hard to walk away." He drew a long breath. "And as much as I want to make you promises, Lindsey, I can't right now."

She loved this man, and right now nothing else mattered but that. "I'm not asking you to, Brady."

"You deserve more. I don't want to leave you, but I committed time to the air force. I could be deployed again."

She hated the fact that she understood. Yet she was afraid for him, too. "That's an excuse, Brady. We all have commitments, but that doesn't mean we can't work out some sort of compromise."

He rested his forehead against hers. "I've got some ghosts to face—obligations." He checked his watch. "I have to go. My flight leaves…"

Lindsey nodded. It took every bit of strength inside her to step back. The air force was his life. Flying was his passion. She'd known that from the start.

With tears blurring her vision, she watched him walk out of her life.

CHAPTER TWELVE

IT WAS more than a week later, just days before Christmas, when Lindsey found herself back in San Angelo. Hank had called and convinced her to stay on as the veterinarian, if only temporarily. Since Brady was gone and she hadn't heard from him, there wasn't any reason she couldn't return to what she loved to do. And with Jack on the mend from his successful transplant, she could leave Ft. Worth.

She walked out onto the porch of the same cabin she'd stayed in before. It was hard to push aside the memories, all the time she and Brady had shared here.

She wanted to forget him, but she loved this man who put duty and love of his country at top priority. She only wanted a small part of his life and for him to let her go with him. Had he been deployed overseas? No matter where he'd gone, there was no denying she loved him.

Lindsey glanced up into the cloudless sky. She hoped he was happy now. She hugged her jacket closer for warmth as she wandered down the path toward the creek. The small herd of mustangs grazed in the golden meadow grass.

She was doing what she loved, too. In a place she'd come to love like a home. Even if she didn't stay on after Dr. Hillman's practice was sold, Hank had invited her to come back periodically and check the ponies.

Hank Barrett hadn't been subtle in trying to convince her to stay permanently. She wanted so much to live here and be around the Randells. To keep that one link between Jack and his sons.

Still she missed Brady, wanted the best for him. "I hope you've banished your ghosts," she whispered into the cool breeze.

"I have, Doc," a familiar voice answered.

She turned around to see Brady on Dusty. He wore his same bomber jacket and cowboy hat. And a silly grin.

She blinked several times, wondering if she'd wanted to see him so badly that she dreamed him up. "Brady? How? You're here?"

He swung his leg over the horse's rump and jumped down. "Surprised?"

"Well, you seem to pop up everywhere." She didn't like this. "Are you home for the holidays?"

"You could say that." He walked toward her. "But mostly I'm here to see you."

"I thought you'd gone back on active duty. Tess said you aced the review board."

"I did. I've even been up in an F-16, and everything went fine. Great, in fact. No more nightmares about the crash. I only dream of you these days."

She refused to get excited. "I'm happy for you."

Brady had been hoping for a friendlier welcome. "I'm glad you came back here, Lindsey. It's where you belong." He moved closer. "I'm selfish, since I like having you around."

She stiffened. "So you think I'm going to be around for your convenience whenever you come home on leave? Well, think again, fly boy. You can just turn around and ride off."

Brady couldn't help but smile. God, he'd missed her. "Never again, Doc. I care too much for you." He tried to reach for her, but she stepped back.

"If you do, then why do you keep coming after me, then leaving me again?" She clenched her fists. "How many times do you expect me to say goodbye to you?"

He sobered. "I'm not saying goodbye, Lindsey. I came by your cabin because I wanted to see you, tell you how I feel."

She bit her lower lip. "We both know how it will turn out," she said, then started up the hill toward the cabin.

Brady tied Dusty's reins to a nearby tree and strode after her. "You aren't even going to hear me out?"

"Why? So you can tell me again how much the military means to you? I know how much, Brady."

"No, Lindsey, you mean more."

She turned around and shouted. "Prove it. Ask me to go with you."

Brady was taken aback by her request. "Okay. Lindsey Stafford, will you go with me?"

She looked shocked, then said, "Yes, Brady. I'll go wherever you go."

He continued up the hill until he stood before her. "You'd do that, Doc? You'd go off with me without knowing what the future holds?"

She nodded slowly. "We'd be together."

"What if I go as close as Laughlin Air Force in Del Rio." He raised an eyebrow. "Or say we only have to go as far as the Rocking R's foreman's cottage? That's where we'll live until I build us a bigger house."

Her pretty green eyes narrowed suspiciously.

He let out a long breath. "In two and a half months I'm resigning from active duty."

She gasped. "No, Brady, you can't do that. You love to fly. And I'd never ask you to give it up."

Fighting his own emotions, he reached for her and pulled her close. "I know you wouldn't. God, that's one of the reasons I love you so much."

She searched his face. "I love you, too. But I can't let you do this."

He placed a finger over her lips. "Listen to me first. I'm not resigning my commission. If I decide to take a flight instructor job at Laughlin we'd be close by in Del Rio. The other choice is that I go into the air force reserves. I still get to fly." He smiled. "I hope you can put up with me being gone one weekend a month and two weeks in the summer."

She finally smiled. "I want you to be happy, Brady."

"I've discovered I'm happy when I'm with you. So I'm leaning toward going into the reserves."

"Then I'm happy, too…as long as I get you the rest of the time, fly boy."

His hold tightened. "If I get you, too." His head lowered and his mouth captured hers. The kiss was tender yet hungry, letting Lindsey know how much he cared and wanted a life with her.

When he broke off the kiss, Brady stepped back and reached into his inside jacket pocket, finding his hands were shaking. "I'd planned to do this tonight over a candlelight dinner, but I can't wait any longer. I want everything settled between us." He kissed her again. "I've asked you to wait too many times." He pulled out a black velvet box and opened it, showing off the pear-shaped diamond in a platinum setting.

Lindsey gasped as Brady got down on one knee.

"God, Lindsey, I love you so much. You've become my heart, my soul. I want us to build a life together. Have kids and raise them here in this valley." He swallowed hard. "Will you marry me?"

"Oh, Brady. Yes, I'll marry you."

He stood and slipped the ring on her finger, then she went into his arms. He kissed her again and again. "It's all going to be so good for us, Doc. I've talked with the other Randells. They want me to be the pilot for a flight service to bring guests to the valley. And if you still want it, you can tell Dr. Hillman that you want to buy his practice."

"Whoa, Brady. Do you have any idea what a veterinarian clinic and practice cost?"

"No, but I have money saved, plus my half of the sale of the valley land to Hank. And besides, you're a wonderful vet, Doc. And it's what you always wanted."

She smiled and touched his face. "You are what I always wanted. A good man who loves me. And a big family to share everything with."

He grinned. "Be careful what you ask for. We've got more family than we know what to do with."

"Oh, no," Lindsey gasped. "Including your niece, Livy. How are you going to tell her that you aren't going to marry her?"

He pulled Lindsey against him. "I'll let her down gently. I'll tell her how much I love you, and she'll understand. And I do love you, Doc."

It was true. Lindsey was the only thing he needed in his life. She was his family. Well, maybe a few Randells thrown in the mix wouldn't hurt.

EPILOGUE

Six months later, spring had come to the valley. Lindsey looked at her parents seated on the cabin porch. They'd rented it during their visit here. The Randells had had to adjust to her parents being around after Lindsey's marriage to Brady. And thanks to the bone marrow from Chance, Jack's leukemia was in remission.

They were all learning that life was fragile.

Jack had been grateful for every day, and for the opportunity to come back to see his sons. Of course, he could never take the place of Hank, but he had never planned to. Lindsey knew Jack had been given a second chance in many things, and he wasn't about to mess it up.

She would never forget her wedding day, having Jack there to give her away, and all the Randells showing up to celebrate their special day.

She'd been Mrs. Brady Randell for only a month, and never realized how much she could love another person. Now they were trying to adjust to their new life together. For the time being, Brady had declined the instructor's job at Laughlin. He'd chosen to resign from active duty and make a permanent home here in the valley.

He had just finished up his two weeks of reserve duty and only returned home yesterday. Lindsey felt the heat rise to her face, recalling how Brady spent most of the night, showing her how much he'd missed her.

She sighed. Marriage was wonderful.

Today they planned to ride with the Randell cousins and Hank to check the mustangs. He'd heard one of the mares had dropped a foal. She wanted to make sure everything was all right. Besides, she enjoyed riding with Brady. It wasn't an F-16, but he'd told her riding around his own ranch with his wife was thrill enough.

As a wedding gift, Brady had bought them two quarter horse yearlings from Chance's breeding stables. His cousin had named the large black stallion Wild Blue Yonder. For Lindsey, a sweet roan filly named Captain's Doc. They'd gotten a reduced family price with the promise that Chance got their first foal, and a discount on Lindsey's veterinarian services.

Right now Dusty and Lady were tied to the post, waiting for everyone. Brady had to go with Luke to the construction site for some final details for this next weekend. They were expecting a large crowd at the Golden Meadow Estates open house.

She glanced up the hill to see Brady's truck pulling up, and a rush of feelings raced through her. He came down the steps toward the cabin, stopping briefly to say hello to her parents. Then he continued toward her.

Brady's excitement grew as he neared, picked her up in his arms and kissed her soundly. "God, I missed you," he groaned.

"We've only been separated an hour."

He kissed her again. "I'm talking about the last two weeks."

"I thought you made up for that last night…and this morning." She smiled. "And again after breakfast."

"Never enough."

Lindsey stepped back. "Well, you're going to have to postpone showing me your undying love, because right now we're supposed to go round up some mustangs."

He reluctantly released her. "Okay, but remember where I left off."

"Not a problem." She looked up toward the cabin and waved at Jack and her mom.

He gripped her hand. "I'm glad your parents could come for a visit. It's good for the cousins, too."

"Were you surprised when Chance asked them here?"

He shook his head. "No. It's time to heal."

"And I think there's a place for all of us here in the valley." She looked at her husband. "I also think your dad would be happy that you and Luke are back here now."

Brady found he had a lot to bc grateful for, starting with the day he woke up in the hospital and found his family…and love.

Up on the hill, Hank sat on his horse, his wife, Ella, next to him on the bay gelding he'd given her on her birthday a few years back.

He rested his arm on the saddle horn and looked down at the valley. A herd of wild ponies were grazing in the serene meadow, unaware that anything was going on. Just as he wanted everything to be. Undisturbed.

"Well, are you happy now?" Ella asked.

He tipped his hat back and grinned. "Yes, I am. It's pretty amazing that I can keep enjoying this place." He glanced toward the cabin and saw Jack and Gail. He never thought he'd see the day that that man would come back here. And Hank couldn't be happier. Chance, Cade and Travis needed this closure to their past. Jarred, Wyatt and Dylan had needed to know their roots, too.

"You've done good, Hank Barrett. Not only did you manage to raise some fine sons, but you've seen to it that these ponies are protected from any harm."

Hank's horse shifted as he looked out over the acres of untouched land. He felt a little selfish to have all this beauty, but it wasn't only for him. "It's just the way it should be. We never should forget our past, and the mustangs were a big part of it."

Several riders began to appear. Chance came from one direction along with Cade and Travis. From the west rode Jarred, Wyatt and Dylan. They met and rode up the rise together. They were a formidable group of men on horseback. Hank glanced back over his shoulder and saw Luke and Tess coming from the direction of the Rocking R. He was touched that they all wanted to help with the mustangs. But he knew his boys loved the ponies.

Something caught his eye, and he turned to the creek to see Brady and Lindsey. "Our family keeps growing."

"With more weddings comes more babies," Ella said excitedly. "I wonder who'll be first among the cousins."

Hank Barrett grinned. "Doesn't matter. I say, bring 'em on. There's plenty of love to go around."

He would teach them about the history of this valley.

How family was the most important thing. And how the Randells and the mustangs could live together in harmony in this special valley for many generations to come.

* * * * *

*Celebrate 60 years of pure reading pleasure
with Harlequin®!*
*Silhouette® Romantic Suspense is celebrating with
the glamour-filled, adrenaline-charged series* LOVE
IN 60 SECONDS *starting in April 2009.*
*Six stories that promise to bring the glitz
of Las Vegas, the danger of revenge, the mystery
of a missing diamond, family scandals and
ripped-from-the-headlines intrigue.
Get your heart racing as love happens
in sixty seconds!*

Enjoy a sneak peek of
USA TODAY *bestselling author Marie Ferrarella's*
*THE HEIRESS'S 2-WEEK AFFAIR
Available April 2009
from Silhouette® Romantic Suspense.*

Eight years ago Matt Shaffer had vanished out of Natalie Rothchild's life, leaving behind a one-line note tucked under a pillow that had grown cold: *I'm sorry, but this just isn't going to work.*

That was it. No explanation, no real indication of remorse. The note had been as clinical and compassionless as an eviction notice, which, in effect, it had been, Natalie thought as she navigated through the morning traffic. Matt had written the note to evict her from his life.

She'd spent the next two weeks crying, breaking down without warning as she walked down the street, or as she sat staring at a meal she couldn't bring herself to eat.

Candace, she remembered with a bittersweet pang, had tried to get her to go clubbing in order to get her to forget about Matt.

She'd turned her twin down, but she did get her act together. If Matt didn't think enough of their relationship to try to contact her, to try to make her understand why he'd changed so radically from lover to stranger, then to hell with him. He was dead to her, she resolved. And he'd remained that way.

Until twenty minutes ago.

The adrenaline in her veins kept mounting.

Natalie focused on her driving. Vegas in the daylight wasn't nearly as alluring, as magical and glitzy as it was after dark. Like an aging woman best seen in soft lighting, Vegas's imperfections were all visible in the daylight. Natalie supposed that was why people like her sister didn't like to get up until noon. They lived for the night.

Except that Candace could no longer do that.

The thought brought a fresh, sharp ache with it.

"Damn it, Candy, what a waste," Natalie murmured under her breath.

She pulled up before the Janus casino. One of the three valets currently on duty came to life and made a beeline for her vehicle.

"Welcome to the Janus," the young attendant said cheerfully as he opened her door with a flourish.

"We'll see," she replied solemnly.

As he pulled away with her car, Natalie looked up at the casino's logo. Janus was the Roman god with two faces, one pointed toward the past, the other facing the future. It struck her as rather ironic, given what she was doing here, seeking out someone from her past in order to get answers so that the future could be settled.

The moment she entered the casino, the Vegas phenomena took hold. It was like stepping into a world where time did not matter or even make an appearance. There was only a sense of "now."

Because in Natalie's experience she'd discovered

that bartenders knew the inner workings of any establishment they worked for better than anyone else, she made her way to the first bar she saw within the casino.

The bartender in attendance was a gregarious man in his early forties. He had a quick, sexy smile, which was probably one of the main reasons he'd been hired. His name tag identified him as Kevin.

Moving to her end of the bar, Kevin asked, "What'll it be, pretty lady?"

"Information." She saw a dubious look cross his brow. To counter that, she took out her badge. Granted she wasn't here in an official capacity, but Kevin didn't need to know that. "Were you on duty last night?"

Kevin began to wipe the gleaming black surface of the bar. "You mean during the gala?"

"Yes."

The smile gracing his lips was a satisfied one. Last night had obviously been profitable for him, she judged. "I caught an extra shift."

She took out Candace's photograph and carefully placed it on the bar. "Did you happen to see this woman there?"

The bartender glanced at the picture. Mild interest turned to recognition. "You mean Candace Rothchild? Yeah, she was here, loud and brassy as always. But not for long," he added, looking rather disappointed. There was always a circus when Candace was around, Natalie thought. "She and the boss had at it and then he had our head of security escort her out."

She latched onto the first part of his statement. "They argued? About what?"

He shook his head. "Couldn't tell you. Too far away for anything but body language," he confessed.

"And the head of security?" she asked.

"He got her to leave."

She leaned in over the bar. "Tell me about him."

"Don't know much," the bartender admitted. "Just that his name's Matt Shaffer. Boss flew him in from L.A., where he was head of security for Montgomery Enterprises."

There was no avoiding it, she thought darkly. She was going to have to talk to Matt. The thought left her cold. "Do you know where I can find him right now?"

Kevin glanced at his watch. "He should be in his office. On the second floor, toward the rear." He gave her the numbers of the rooms where the monitors that kept watch over the casino guests as they tried their luck against the house were located.

Taking out a twenty, she placed it on the bar. "Thanks for your help."

Kevin slipped the bill into his vest pocket. "Any time, lovely lady," he called after her. "Any time."

She debated going up the stairs, then decided on the elevator. The car that took her up to the second floor was empty. Natalie stepped out of the elevator, looked around to get her bearings and then walked toward the rear of the floor.

"Into the Valley of Death rode the six hundred," she silently recited, digging deep for a line from a poem by Tennyson. Wrapping her hand around a brass handle, she opened one of the glass doors and walked in.

The woman whose desk was closest to the door looked up. "You can't come in here. This is a restricted area."

Natalie already had her ID in her hand and held it up. "I'm looking for Matt Shaffer," she told the woman.

God, even saying his name made her mouth go dry. She was supposed to be over him, to have moved on with her life. What happened?

The woman began to answer her. "He's—"

"Right here."

The deep voice came from behind her. Natalie felt every single nerve ending go on tactical alert at the same moment that all the hairs at the back of her neck stood up. Eight years had passed, but she would have recognized his voice anywhere.

* * * * *

Why did Matt Shaffer leave heiress-turned-cop
Natalie Rothchild?
What does he know about the death
of Natalie's twin sister?
Come and meet these two reunited lovers and learn
the secrets of the Rothchild family in
THE HEIRESS'S 2-WEEK AFFAIR
by USA TODAY bestselling author
Marie Ferrarella.
The first book in Silhouette® Romantic Suspense's
wildly romantic new continuity,
LOVE IN 60 SECONDS!
Available April 2009.

CELEBRATE
60 YEARS
OF PURE READING PLEASURE
WITH **HARLEQUIN**®!

Look for Silhouette®
Romantic Suspense in April!

Love In 60 Seconds

Bright lights. Big city. Hearts in overdrive.

Silhouette® Romantic Suspense is celebrating
Harlequin's 60th Anniversary with six stories that
promise to bring readers the glitz of Las Vegas,
the danger of revenge, the mystery of a missing
diamond, and family scandals.